RECKONING

DON'T MISS THESE
ALEX ANDER THRILLERS!

Alex Ander writes what he enjoys reading – action thrillers packed with fistfights, gunfights, good-and-decent main characters, and heart-pounding excitement and adventure...all with clean language, no graphic sex, and an undertone of faith from a Christian worldview.

Aaron Hardy – Ex-Special Forces

The Unsanctioned Patriot

American Influence

Deadly Assignment

Patriot Assassin

The Nemesis Protocol

Necessary Means

Foreign Soil

Of Patriots and Tyrants

Act of Justice

The Last Kill

Two Minutes to War

Three Days in Rome

Dark Days of the Republic

Act of War

———————

BIG SKY Series – Sheriff Wade Lockhart

Big Sky

Ambush

Reckoning

Jacob St. Christopher – Former FBI Hostage Rescue
Protect & Defend
Word of Honor
A Vow to the Innocent
Above & Beyond
Hard Road to Redemption

Jaxon Reigns – Ex-CIA Paramilitary Operations
To Reign Supreme
Hard Reign

Special Agent Cruz – FBI Agent
Vengeance is Mine
Defense of Innocents
Plea for Justice

Jessica Devlin – U.S. Marshal
Trust Fall
No Good Options
Let the Hunt Begin

Other Action Thrillers
Kill Order
Far From Mercy
Executive One Foxtrot

FREE Ebook
Escape & Evade
Go to AlexAnderNovelist.com

RECKONING

MODERN SHERIFF CRIME THRILLER

ALEX ANDER

This book is a work of fiction. All names, characters, places and incidents are the products of the author's imagination or are used fictitiously. Any similarities to real events or locations or actual persons, living or dead, is entirely coincidental.

TABLE OF CONTENTS

"For I know well the plans
I have in mind for you,
plans for your welfare and not for woe,
so as to give you a future of hope."
~ *Jeremiah Chapter 29; Verse 11*

RECKONING

CHAPTER 1
LEVER GUNS & CAR SEATS

It wasn't even halfway through January, and every day of the month had seen snowfall in Big Sky County. Some days brought several inches, while other days saw only a dusting or flurries. In addition to the white stuff collecting on roadways and sidewalks and being shoveled into piles everywhere, the temperatures had been colder than normal. Low twenties had been the daytime highs with most nights seeing single digits on average. Hardened county residents, many of whom had lived in Big Sky their whole lives, hadn't experienced weather this cold and snowy in a long time.

Its windshield wipers going, clearing away what seemed like a constant snowfall, the boxy, old-style hunter-green Jeep Grand Wagoneer, wood-grained panels on its sides and tailgate, rolled over the freshly deposited three inches of snow, bypassing citizens of Wyatt, Montana, who were making their way from one warm building to another or to their vehicles. Most people had their hands full or were snuggling up to whoever was with them, each person shielding the other from a bitter wind. Those unlucky enough to be traveling solo just put their heads down and speed walked to their destination.

Inside the Grand Wagoneer, 45-year-old Big Sky County Sheriff Wade Lockhart spun the steering wheel to the right and navigated the SUV into a parking spot across from the sheriff's office.

Located on Main Street, in the center of Wyatt, the redbrick building had once been a post office. Then, after a gun store had occupied the structure for a few years, it became available again after the firearm business had gone bankrupt. Now, for the past six months, it had been the new headquarters for the Big Sky Sheriff's Office.

Lockhart shut off the engine, climbed out, and opened the right rear door. After spending the next few minutes hunched over and fiddling with something, he backed out and slung a lever action rifle over his left shoulder, muzzle pointing upward.

"Hi, Sheriff."

Lockhart turned to see one of Big Sky's newest residents, Kristina Walters. The two had crossed paths back in October when he had been investigating his son Jace's murder. Lockhart recalled his first meeting with the twenty-eight-year-old, five-nothing slender woman who, at that time, had been working as a hooker, and as a dancer at a strip club in Roseburg, Idaho. Her face had sported every imaginable kind of makeup known to mankind—mascara, rouge, eyeliner, eye shadow, lipstick, all of it.

          RECKONING

Now he saw a woman who had traded in her face paint, miniskirts, and five-inch spiked heels for—he gave her outfit a quick peek—for ankle-high black winter boots, blue jeans, a long dark-gray winter coat, and what looked like a hand-knitted red stocking cap. Her long, black curly hair stuck out from under the covering. *Yup,* he thought. *A real Montanan.* "Tina," he replied. Since moving to Montana, she had started going by 'Tina.' *A new start deserves a new name,* she had told him.

"I can't believe how cold it is here," she said.

He eyeballed her rosy cheeks, thin face, brown eyes, and long lashes, lashes that appeared to have a modest amount of mascara on them. He thought of his deceased wife. Outside of a light layer of mascara, Cheryl had never worn makeup a day in her life, at least never in all the days he had known her. *I'm a natural beauty,* she had joked.

Lockhart thought of Sierra, his girlfriend. She too hadn't worn any makeup in the short time the two had been together. Perhaps that was what had caught his eye when he first met her. Whether or not he knew it, he had always been attracted to women who didn't cover up their faces but let their true nature shine. Inwardly shaking his head to drag himself away from the mental sidebar his thoughts had gone down, he focused on Tina. "Yes, it's definitely been a cold one." He poked his chin at her. "How are you settling in here? How's the job going?"

Through his undersheriff, Lockhart had discovered

Tina had worked as a vet assistant and had been going to school to become a veterinary technician before her life fell apart, and she soon found herself stripping and hooking to pay the bills. He hadn't been told the entire story about what had happened to her; however, his undersheriff had said something about Tina being shunned by her parents, by her religion. But he didn't need to know the gritty details to know he wanted to help her. So, he had acted, serving as a liaison between Tina and Big Sky's only veterinarian, a man who had been searching for someone to help him with the mundane chores around the clinic: administering medication, bathing animals, collecting samples, cleaning the facilities, tasks like that.

Lockhart had paid Tina's travel expenses and set her up in a motel, so she could get a feel for Wyatt, see if the town was a good fit for her. During her stay, she had interviewed with the veterinarian and was offered the job. The pay wasn't great, but she had a little money saved up. Between her savings, a two-week advance on her salary, and a promise from Lockhart that he'd kick in some financial help if she needed it, Tina had decided to make the jump and move to Wyatt, Montana.

"The job is great," said a beaming Tina. "I love working with animals again. There're no lies, no deceit with them. You know exactly what you're getting." She reached out and squeezed his forearm. "I can't thank you enough for everything you've done for me, Sheriff, getting me this job, helping me move here."

He raised a hand. "I may have greased the wheels, but you still had to put in the hard work."

"I know, but if you hadn't knocked on my door that night, I'd still be," she stopped short, "well, you know what I'd still be doing."

"That's all in the past." He gave Wyatt a glance then came back to her. "You're one of us now. We take care of our own."

She pointed at him. "That reminds me. I have some money for you, but," she made a face, "I'm afraid I left it at home."

Lockhart had paid the deposit and part of her first month's rent payment. He waved her off. "Don't worry about it."

"That's the thing. I *do* worry about it. I pay my debts," she smiled again, "especially to those who've done so much for me."

He regarded her bright, cheery, youthful countenance. *She looks so much younger without all that junk on her face.* "I'm just glad I could help."

Tina checked her watch. "I have to get to work, but," she faced him, "if you're going to be around this afternoon, I could get the money during my lunch hour and drop it off to you."

"That would be fine, but really," he pumped a hand her way, "there's no rush."

She wiped a gloved hand over her face, to clear away

some snow, then pressed her lips together and gave him a long, tender look. "You're one of the nicest men I know, you know that?"

"Thank you."

She came in for a quick hug then backed away. "Okay, well…I better let you go." She waved, "Bye, Sheriff," then continued down the sidewalk toward the clinic.

He watched her leave, inwardly pleased she was getting her life on track again. *God be praised.* He retrieved a car seat from the Jeep, shut the door with his foot, and strolled around the right-front bumper, his lever gun still hanging off his left shoulder. Holding the small car seat in his right hand, a thick blanket completely covering the portable seat, the six-one, one-sixty Lockhart looked like he was getting ready to do a bicep curl as he stepped off the sidewalk. He paused and frowned. *God be praised?* He glanced down. *When have I ever thought that before?*

Moments later, he shook his head and hurried across the street. His black Ariat pull-on work boots crunched snow underfoot. His black Resistol fur felt cattleman-crown cowboy hat and black mid-thigh leather fringe jacket—with all the fringe having been cut off immediately after purchase—were gathering a layer of tiny snowflakes. Blue jeans rounded out his attire.

An oncoming truck slowed.

Lockhart pulled up.

          RECKONING

An arm emerged from behind the driver's rolled-down window, and a man waved, then motioned.

Lockhart waved back then crossed the street. Passing through two sets of double doors, he entered the empty main lobby of the sheriff's office. Black leather chairs sat side by side on the walls to the left and right. Among the chairs, several two-foot-square low tables were strategically placed to allow visitors to set beverages or other items down. Overhead, tube lighting cast a bright 5000 Kelvin hue over the entire area. Gray tile floors throughout met up with small, carpeted sections where the chairs and tables were.

Lockhart strolled down the tiled 'runway' to a four-foot-high redbrick wall that bisected the lobby from administration and the deputies' cubicles. Above the wall, glass rose to the ten-foot-high, tiled ceiling. Two, five-by-two-foot dark oak wooden saloon doors were positioned at the brick wall's horizontal halfway point, a foot off the floor and right in line with the front doors.

He pushed on the left door and walked into the admin section, leading with the car seat.

The door swung by the other one, swung back inside, then repeated the process a couple times before settling.

Seated at her desk on the right, right next to the brick wall, 38-year-old Bristol Mackenzie looked up, a headset arched over her long blonde hair pulled up into a messy bun. She wore light-red rectangular eyeglasses that matched the red ribbon holding her hair up. Cocking her head and frowning at the 'package' her boss was carrying, she spoke into the boom microphone that ran from the headset to her mouth. "Yes, we need them delivered sooner rather than later."

On his twelve o'clock, just outside the door to his office on the left, 35-year-old Piper Jennings pecked away at her computer.

"Morning, Piper," he said.

She shot him a quick look then went back to her task. "Good morning, W—" she did a double-take at the 'package' he was carrying before her brows came together, "ade."

Lockhart ducked into his office.

Dressed in blue jeans, a tan-colored official uniform shirt, sleeves rolled up to her elbows, the five-six, 125-pound undersheriff stood and pointed brown cowboy boots toward Lockhart's open office. Plopping hands onto the gun belt that held her Glock 19, magazine pouches, two-way radio, handcuffs, and other tools of her trade, she turned toward Bristol, her scowl deepening.

The two women exchanged similar expressions.

"Thank you. I appreciate you looking into this," said Bristol before tapping her headset a moment later while marching toward Piper.

Sporting straight, shoulder-length dirty blonde hair, blue eyes, a narrow, slightly upturned nose, prominent chin, and a beauty mark an inch from the right corner of her wide-lipped mouth, Piper ambled into the sheriff's office.

Two beats later, showing off black jeans, red faux snakeskin square-toed cowboy boots, and a white blouse, Bristol arrived to stand on Piper's right. Both women watched Lockhart pull back a blanket and extract a baby from the car seat.

Half grinning, he sat in his chair, crossed his legs, ankle on knee, and cradled the baby in his lap.

The women gave each other another look before Piper opened her mouth to show off white teeth, a noticeable gap between her two upper front teeth. "Um," she folded her arms across her chest, "help me out here, Wade. The math isn't adding up. You and Sierra have only been seeing each other for a couple of months now, so-o-o," she held out her hands, palms up, "is there something you want to tell us?"

He frowned while looking away from the women, pretending to be thinking. "No, I," he paused, "I don't think so. Oh, wait." He dipped his forehead toward the rifle on the other side of his desk. "I did want to ask if you'd clean my Henry there. I put some rounds through it yesterday and haven't had time to clean it yet."

Simultaneously, Piper and Bristol made a show of crossing their arms in front of them while each cocked her head at him.

Following another five seconds of keeping a straight face, he smiled, "Oh, you're wondering about," he held up the baby, "*this* young man." He spent the next minute giving them a shortened version of what had happened, then finished with, "His name is Jace Wade Lockhart."

Both women looked on, their mouths hanging open. A tick later, after recovering, they raced toward Lockhart's desk, Piper pulling into the lead at the last moment.

Thinking he had seen an elbow or two thrown, he smiled inwardly before motioning toward his Henry. "The gun's right there, Piper."

"Clean your own rifle." She reached out with both hands. "Gimme. Gimme. I want baby."

Chuckling, he forfeited his grandson.

"Ooh," Piper cooed. "You are such a beautiful thing. You know that?" She bounced slightly while rocking Jace Wade. "Oh, I can see your daddy's sparkling blue eyes." She did a one-eighty and headed for the doorway. "You're going to be a heartbreaker, too, aren't you?"

"So, you're not going to clean my rifle?" asked Lockhart.

Piper cranked her head around. "You *know* I'll clean it," she went back to Jace Wade, "right after I've had my fill of baby." She pretended to take a couple bites of the infant. "You're so delicious. I'm going to eat you up. Yes, I am." She waggled her head at the boy. "Yes, I am."

"Don't go too far with him, Piper," said Bristol. "I'm next."

"Catch me if you can," retorted the undersheriff while leaving Lockhart's office.

Bristol shook her head then turned back toward a smiling Lockhart. She took in his short, light-brown hair, sky-blue eyes, and long eyelashes.

He noticed her grinning at him, her head tipped to one side as she held the tip of one of her eyeglasses' temples inside pursed lips. "What?" he said.

"I haven't seen you like this since before," becoming stoic, she hesitated, glanced down, then faced him again, her pleased countenance returning. "It's good to see you smiling again, Wade."

He nodded. "Thanks, Bristol."

"I realize things still have to be pretty fresh, but," she rocked her head backward, "I'm sure he's going to be a real blessing in your life. I'm really glad you have him."

Lockhart eyed the doorway, his ears picking up a cooing Piper outside. "So am I." A moment. "So am I."

"Well," his secretary put her spectacles back on, "before I go cut in out there, I wanted to tell you that that lawyer called for you again this morning." The attorney had called three times yesterday. Each time, Lockhart had told Bristol to tell him he wasn't in. "Thankfully, this time," continued Bristol, "I could *honestly* say you weren't in."

He nodded.

"The guy's just going to keep calling, Wade. Those people don't give up."

"Battle of wills, I guess."

She rolled her eyes. "And knowing how strong *your*

will is," a beat, "I'll be lying to him until his client is put to death."

He curled up one side of his mouth. "At least you know there's an end in sight."

• • •

For the last five minutes, Piper had fielded incoming calls for Bristol, so the latter woman could hold the baby.

"Thank you for watching him overnight," said Kinsley. At a hundred pounds, 20-year-old Kinsley Harris had a skinny, five-one build. She had long black straight hair with straight bangs down to her thin eyebrows. Her pale white skin was speckled with brown freckles on her cheeks and nose, and she had a smallish head, petite chin, and narrow lips. "I can't tell you how good it felt to get a full night's sleep. I hope he was good for you."

"He fussed for a bit," replied Lockhart, "but Jace used to do the same thing at that age. His mother would sing him this song while I rubbed his belly." Lockhart barely shook his head. "Didn't take long, and he was sleeping peacefully."

Smiling at the story, Kinsley cocked her head at Lockhart. "You'll have to teach me that song."

"I was never the singing type. That was all Cheryl."

Kinsley pressed her lips together then nodded abruptly. "I should probably get going. JW has a checkup later this morning."

RECKONING

"Well," Bristol handed off the baby, "if you ever need a sitter, all you have to do is ask."

"That goes for me, too," said Piper, stepping away from the front desk and approaching the gathering. She beamed at the baby. "I'd watch you anytime." Her eyes big, she gave Jace Wade a broad, toothy smile. "Yes, I would, you sweet little thing you."

Kinsley placed Jace Wade in the car seat and wrapped him in the blanket. "Well, if my," she stood tall and regarded Lockhart, "semi," she tilted her head at the man, "sort of...father-in-law says it's okay," her brows up, she studied him.

Lockhart looked up from the car seat to meet Kinsley's gaze. He nodded, "I trust them," then went back to gazing at his grandson.

Kinsley's shoulders drooped a bit, and she lost some of her radiance.

Bristol's eyes shifted from the girl to her boss to the girl again.

Recovering, Kinsley picked up the car seat, covered Jace Wade with another blanket, and gave the women a crisp, forced smile. "Thank you for the offer. I might just take you up on that." A beat. "It was nice meeting you both."

Bristol: "You too."

Piper: "Likewise."

Kinsley faced Lockhart and raised a tentative hand. "Bye, Sheriff."

He nodded once. "Drive safely."

"I will." She pushed her way through the saloon doors and entered the cold weather a few steps later.

A grinning Piper slapped Lockhart on the arm on her way toward his office. "I better see to cleaning that rifle of yours."

"Thanks, Piper." He gaped through all the glass windows between him and Main Street, his eyes on the car seat, as Kinsley skirted across the street and made a left, leaving his vision a second later.

"Wade, you do know that girl's reaching out to you, right?" said Bristol.

Lockhart faced his secretary, his brows inching closer together.

"Didn't you see her heart sink when you didn't respond to her father-in-law comment?"

He scratched his chin while turning his head to squint at the street outside.

"Now, I don't know her family situation," continued Bristol, "but it was clear she's definitely trying to find out where she stands with *you*."

"She did mention she spent four years in foster care after her parents died. And that JW has no one alive on *her* side of the family."

A frustrated Bristol looked at the ceiling while pumping open hands in the air before backhanding him in the upper arm. "See? That poor girl is all alone in the world with a newborn baby. She's probably scared out of her wits, trying to figure out how she's going to do everything all by herself."

Lockhart came back to Bristol. "She's the mother of my grandson and someone who was obviously important to Jace. Of course, she can count on me to help her out."

"Have you *said* that to her?"

He half closed one eye at the street again.

Bristol raised a corner of her mouth and shook her head at him. "You're so much like my father. He, too, had a heart of gold. He'd do anything for us kids, but to have a heartfelt conversation with the man? Nope. Wasn't going to happen. Eventually, my siblings and I realized what he *said* wasn't what mattered. What mattered was what he *did*."

Lockhart chewed over her words. She wasn't all that far off. There were only two people he had ever opened up to—his mother and his wife. They were gone now, though. And on some level, they had taken with them his desire to share feelings with anyone else. Plus, let's face it. He was a man, and most men didn't share feelings. Lockhart squinted. *This one didn't, anyway.*

"Look," resumed Bristol, "all I'm—"

A phone rang.

She shot a glance toward her desk then started backing away from Lockhart. "You're a bright guy, Wade. Pay attention to the signs, and you'll see what I'm seeing." Bristol turned her back on him while tapping her headset. "Sheriff's Office. Big Sky County. Bristol speaking."

Lockhart folded arms across his chest, cupping his right elbow while stroking his chin with his right hand. Bristol's words played again in his mind. *She's definitely trying to find out where she stands with you.*

"Let me see if he's in," said Bristol before she tapped her headset and eyed her boss. "Wade, it's that lawyer guy."

He spied his secretary.

She cocked her head at him while arching her brows. It was a classic 'what do you want me to do?' look.

But the sheriff side of him saw something entirely different in her eyes. They were pleading with him to take the call, to save her from having to play gatekeeper. He ran his tongue over his lower teeth a few times, grimaced, then jerked his head toward his office, "Send him to me," before he strolled toward his workplace, rubbing the back of his neck.

Bristol's voice: "You're in luck, sir. He's in. I'm transferring you now."

• • •

Five Minutes Later...

While putting on his leather jacket, Lockhart marched out of his office. "Bristol?"

She faced him.

"Push my morning appointments to the afternoon."

He flattened his coat's collar. "If I need to cancel them later, I'll call."

"Um," she sat upright in her chair, "okay." A tick. "Where are you off to in such a hurry?"

Sticking out an arm ahead of him, "To meet with my son's murderer," he barged through the saloon doors.

NINETY MINUTES LATER
HALLIE, MONTANA
MONTANA STATE CORRECTIONAL FACILITY

Located twenty-five miles outside of Big Sky County, to the northwest, Montana State Correctional Facility sat on a 75-acre compound flanked by mountains on three sides. A modern prison, MSCF provided low to high security levels for 1,500 male inmates. And one of its newest arrivals was Davis Bronson.

The meeting room at MSCF was a step up from the usual law enforcement interrogation rooms. The lighting was better. The chairs were more comfortable. And the one-way mirror was replaced with a window that overlooked an interior section of the facility. Finally, there were two access doors, one led deeper into the facility while the other was for visitors, attorneys, anyone coming in from outside the prison.

Lockhart stood behind a couple of 'construction orange,' padded plastic chairs. In the five minutes he had been waiting, he was doubting his coming here. What could Davis Bronson offer him? The man's corpse? That would be a great start. But since he had made the drive, he might as well hear out the criminal.

The gray metal door leading deeper into the prison opened.

Wearing handcuffs, a belly chain, and leg irons, Davis Bronson shuffled into the room ahead of a corrections officer who instructed the prisoner to sit in one of two plastic chairs at a six-foot-long table across from Lockhart.

Bronson sat.

The CO secured Bronson's leg irons to a bolt sunk into the floor, removed the man's handcuffs, then left the room as the door leading to the 'outside' swung open.

A short man in his early thirties, wearing a black suit, white shirt, and blue tie, entered carrying a dark-brown leather briefcase. His shoes and belt matched his briefcase. "I appreciate you meeting with us, Sheriff Lockhart," said the man while extending his right hand toward Lockhart. "Myles Tanner, Mr. Bronson's attorney.

A good seven inches taller, Lockhart looked down at the man and took in black and short 'spikey' hair, dark-colored eyes, wide-spaced eyebrows, and a chubby red face. After giving the man's hand a fair bit of scrutiny, he half-heartedly shook it.

Filling out his suit, the two-hundred-pound man huffed while rounding the table and setting his briefcase on the furniture's surface. "Mr. Bronson."

Bronson said nothing, didn't even acknowledge the man. He simply sat there, inwardly seething at the one who had put him in this place.

Lockhart squinted at the two-inch-long cut on Bronson's left cheek, compliments of the three-pound Ruger Redhawk Lockhart had used as a hammer on the man's face during their struggle in Wyoming. He then recalled seeing the hitch in Bronson's gait when the man had entered the room. "How's the leg? I saw you limping." In that same fight, the sheriff had stuck his Buck 110 Hunter Sport knife's 3.75-inch, clip-point blade into the man's left thigh.

Not about to give the sheriff any satisfaction, the inmate said nothing.

"Okay," said Tanner, taking the seat on his client's right while motioning toward the chair ahead of Lockhart, "shall we get started?"

Lockhart remained standing, his focus on the man who had murdered his son. Back in Wyoming, he had come within a hair of pulling the trigger on his Ruger and sending a 240-grain 44 Magnum bullet into Bronson's mouth. He still didn't know what had kept him from doing so. And now that he was face to face with Jace's killer, the itch to finish what he had started had crept back into his psyche. He pressed his right elbow to his side but didn't feel the butt of the Redhawk. Fortunately for Bronson, Lockhart had to leave his revolver 'at the door' before proceeding further into the facility. "Why am I here?"

Seeing his invitation to sit had not been accepted, Tanner nodded, "As you wish, Sheriff," before thumbing open his briefcase's latches, opening the carry case, and withdrawing a piece of paper. "Before we get to that, I've taken the liberty of drafting a letter from you." He slid the paper across the table. "My client is requesting clemency, and we think your testimony would prove vital in obtaining that clemency from the courts."

Lockhart picked up the sheet and perused it. He couldn't believe what he was reading. If he hadn't known better, he would have thought he was reading a letter of recommendation he had written for a close friend. He glimpsed Bronson then stared at the man's attorney. "You want me to recommend the judge take the death penalty off the table? Is this a joke?"

"Not at all, Sheriff," said Tanner. "What my client has to offer will be very important to you. We're simply asking for a little something in return. That's all. Once you," he motioned toward the paper Lockhart held, "sign that, my client is willing to tell you everything he knows."

Lockhart flicked the document toward the table. "Nothing is worth letting this," he scowled at Bronson, "puke off from getting what he deserves."

"Even if," said the one in chains, "I could lead you to the man behind your son's murder?"

Through narrow slits for eyes, Lockhart glared at Bronson. "I'm *looking* at that man right now. This was a waste of time," he added while striding toward the door.

"I didn't say the man who *killed* your son. I said..."

Lockhart reached for the doorknob.

"...the man *behind* your son's murder."

Lockhart froze, his hand in midair, his fingers inches from the round, brass-colored handle. A few seconds later, he spun back toward Bronson. "What are you saying?" He understood the nuances between 'killed' and 'behind,' but he wanted to hear it out loud.

Bronson donned a smirk and leaned back in his chair. "Do you think I just decided to up and blow your kid's brains out along the side of the road?"

Lockhart made fists while lowering his head to glare at Bronson from just under his brows.

Tanner saw the anger flash across the sheriff's face. He leaned closer to his client. "Perhaps a little decorum is in order here, Mr. Bronson."

Bronson thrust his chin toward the man representing him. "You can," he cursed, "your decorum." A beat. "And you can," he used the same curse word again, "*you too*, while you're at it." He faced the lawman. "This is a business deal. I have something you want, and you'll have to pony up to get it."

Casting glances at the other men, Tanner squirmed in his chair.

"So, what's it going to be, Mister Sheriff?" Bronson leaned forward and rested forearms on the table, interlacing his fingers a tick later. "Are you really that interested in seeing me fry that you'd let the man—the one who *ordered* the hit on your kid—go unpunished?"

Lockhart set his jaw. Could this really be true? Was

there a contract put out on Jace? If so, why? Or was this Bronson's way of saving himself from the death penalty? Thinking, Lockhart ground his teeth together. He knew if he didn't see this through, sign that document, he would never stop wondering if there was more to his son's murder. He strolled back to the table, slid the paper toward himself, and held out his left hand toward Tanner.

The man offered a pen.

Lockhart scribbled above his printed name, tossed the pen across the table, then stood.

Both Tanner and Bronson reached for the paper.

Lockhart reversed course and laid both hands on the table, his left one squarely on the page, while his eyes settled on Bronson. "Not until I get what I want." A pulse. "Talk."

Bronson went from the sheriff to the paper to the sheriff again. "Once I tell you, you could just tear it up."

"You're right." He sneered at the man, envisioning himself reaching out with both hands and twisting this guy's head right off. "Talk."

Bronson breathed in, his focus on the white sheet pinned to the table. Moments later, he grimaced then exhaled while glancing up at Lockhart. "By now, I'm sure you know about the robbery," he rolled a finger, "the old man with the guns, the ones we were supposed to steal?"

Lockhart nodded.

"Yeah, there was never any robbery that was

supposed to take place. That was all a ruse to get Bartlett on board, so he would line up our getaway car."

Roger Bartlett. Lockhart recalled the man who had been in the backseat of the sedan the night of Jace's murder. "Go on."

"Nick and I," Nick Castellano, Bronson's partner, "we had been scoping out the target for a few days."

Lockhart's muscles tensed upon him hearing his son being referred to as a 'target.'

"We waited for when we knew he was going to be driving around. Timed it just right and sped by him doing ninety. He pulled us over, and, well," Bronson curled up one side of his mouth, "you know the rest."

Lockhart squinted at Bronson. The urge to snap the man's neck had returned. "Who ordered the hit on my son?"

"I can't tell you that."

Lockhart stood tall and made ready to rip the sheet in half.

"Wait, wait, wait," blurted Bronson, his eyes glued to his 'lifeline.' "But I can give you the name of the man who hired us."

Lockhart cocked his head and raised his brows, waiting.

"Pete '*Petey*' McCord."

"And why did this Pete McCord want my son dead?"

Bronson shrugged. "Don't know. Don't care. He gave me money to do a job, and I did the job. But I can tell you this, though. Petey *wasn't* the one who ordered the hit."

"A go-between?"

Bronson nodded. "There's no way that guy put out the hit."

"What makes you say that?"

"Please." Bronson looked offended. "When you've been doing this as long as I have, you get to know who the *players* are and who the *chumps* are. This guy was definitely a *chump*."

"And how do I find this chump?" asked Lockhart.

Bronson gave up an address then gestured toward the 'recommendation' letter. "So, are you going to give that back?"

Lockhart folded the paper twice, making it the size of a standard envelope. "Depends."

"On what?" prodded Bronson. "I told you everything I know. I'm not lying. I swear."

"If that's true," tucking the folded sheet into an inner jacket pocket, "and I find whoever took out a contract on my son," Lockhart walked away, "then you'll see me again." He opened the door and left the room.

•••

Fifteen Minutes Later...

Holding his cell phone to his right cheek, Lockhart checked his side-view mirror, stepped on the accelerator, and eased the Jeep Grand Wagoneer onto the expressway. "If what Bronson says is true, then this changes everything." Minutes ago, after having driven through the prison gates, he had called Piper to bring her up to speed and have her direct him to Pete McCord's place. "You're going to need to go back six months, maybe more, and really dig deep into Jace's reports."

Distracted, she replied, "Okay."

"Discount nothing or no one. It may sound crazy, but at this point, even a traffic stop may be beneficial to us."

"Okay, I got it. Are you ready to take down McCord's address?"

"Go."

"Once you exit the interstate, you turn—this would be a whole lot easier, Wade, if you'd just get a smartphone."

"Why? I have *you*."

She sighed. "If you had a smartphone, I could send you the route," she continued, "or better yet, you could enter the address yourself, and you'd have step-by-step directions right there with you."

"You said I turn *which* way once I leave the interstate?"

Following another low groan, Piper relayed the directions, then added, "Do you really think Bronson's telling the truth? I mean, the guy's a cold-blooded murderer. Lying to get out of being executed isn't a stretch at all for someone like that."

"I won't know that until I question this Pete McCord fellow."

"You know, I'm only about forty-five—"

"No," said Lockhart.

"You don't even know what I was going to say," she said.

"You want to be there when I visit McCord."

"Okay, so you *did* know what I was going to say."

"For the time being, we need to divide our forces to cover more ground. And I need you *there*, looking into all things related to Jace. He's your top priority. If something else comes up, something that can't wait, call in a deputy to deal with it."

"All right." She huffed. "I will."

Hearing the concern in her voice, he half grinned inside, knowing how she had casually taken up the mantle of looking after him after his wife had passed away. He didn't mind, though. In fact, he had probably needed a little looking after during those earlier years. "Don't worry, Piper. I'll be just fine." He closed his phone and focused on the road.

Lockhart stopped the Grand Wagoneer in front of a stone driveway on his right, where two trailers sat with molded covers protecting them from the elements. Parked end to end, the nearest one appeared to be a utility trailer, while the other was much bigger. That one was in the size category of a tow-behind camper.

Downtown Adder, Montana, population nine thousand, was another five miles west of this little offshoot of a community. Here, the one and two-story houses—most with vinyl siding exteriors, a few sporting redbrick—were nicely built, with plenty of surrounding property and tall trees. They were far enough away from each other to afford homeowners privacy while remaining within 'snooping' distance.

Lockhart's gaze took him left of, and beyond, the covered trailers. Pete McCord's house was a modest, one-story home with white vinyl siding, green trim, and gray shingles. To the left of the structure sat a three-car garage with siding, trim, and shingles that matched those elements of the house. Three tall pines, their boughs bending upward and holding snow, lined the left side of the main driveway on the left side of the front lawn. A single-lane dirt driveway ran to the garage, widening at the garage to allow four vehicles to be parked side by side.

Lockhart zeroed in on a black, four-door SUV parked facing the garage door. Piper had called him while he had been on the road. One of the things she had discovered was that McCord drove a black, four-door GMC Yukon.

The Big Sky sheriff looked over his right shoulder, toward the east, to see the mostly wooded terrain between McCord's place and the nearest cross street covered in snow. In fact, this whole area was blanketed by a fresh coat of the 'white stuff.' Presently, however, the falling snow had stopped, and the clouds were breaking up. Pivoting back to his left, he saw a redbrick home, fifty yards to the west of McCord's.

Across the street, on his ten o'clock, situated a hundred yards off the road, a two-story yellow house with a brown roof sat at the end of an asphalt driveway. A chain-link fence surrounded the property while a brown, wooden, three-rail horse fence ran straight back from the road where it joined a matching perpendicular fence. To the left of the fence, a black horse stood near a small outbuilding, chewing on hay, as it stared at the newcomer. Lockhart squinted at the animal. From this distance, a good seventy-five yards away, he estimated it to be no more than fifteen hands high. And judging from its apparent chubbiness and smallish legs, he guessed it to be a quarter horse.

Rotating his head and shoulders further left, Lockhart spied a shuddered building on his seven o'clock. The structure, once having been a small convenience store, sat a hundred yards away and fifty feet off the road.

Lockhart took his foot off the brake pedal, and the Jeep rolled to the other side of the main driveway. He parked the vehicle on the street and activated its emergency flashers.

Strolling up the driveway, he noted squiggly tire ruts in the snow that became straighter the closer they got to the garage. Following a quick examination of the ruts, he deduced they had come from a second vehicle that had been parked alongside McCord's SUV. Multiple tracks in the snow were littered in the space between the driveway and the back of the house.

Lockhart veered right, took three steps to a porch, then knocked on the front door. On the third rap, the metal door swung inward an inch, and the skin on his neck tingled. "Pete McCord? Sheriff's Office."

No reply.

"Mr. McCord, Sheriff Lockhart."

Nothing.

Drawing his Ruger Redhawk, "Mr. McCord, I'm coming in," Lockhart pushed open the door and entered.

Just inside the doorway, a man lay on his back, arms and legs splayed, his eyes gaping at the ceiling. His royal-blue bathrobe was cinched but had opened at the waist to show off his legs and genitals.

Lockhart checked for a pulse while keeping his attention, and the Ruger, on the rest of the living room. *Dead.*

He stood and inspected the area, his attention drawn to a bowl resting on a small table beside the door. Inside the bowl were car keys, a pocketknife, and loose change. He pushed those items aside to get to a thin metal object at the bottom. Flipping open the silver case, which he recognized as one of those RFID-blocking credit card holders, he found a driver's license identifying the man on the floor as Peter A. McCord of Adder, Montana.

With his Redhawk in both hands, Lockhart searched the kitchen then headed down a short hallway with two doors on the right and one on the left.

Ambient light from a living room floor lamp cast a dim glow down the hallway and into the first room on the right.

Plucking his Pelican 2360 flashlight from a pants pocket, he held it in his left hand—above his head and to the left—while peeking around the corner to light up the room before quickly retreating. He reversed course, ducked into the room, and pointed both light and revolver throughout an empty bedroom.

Crossing the hall, he eased open a door and repeated the same clearing process again in an empty bathroom.

Finally, at the end of the hall, on the right, he put the backs of his hands together and aimed both flashlight and gun into the corner room. Slowly, 'slicing the pie,' he cleared the room then holstered his Ruger.

Locating a light switch, he flicked it on to see that he was standing inside a bedroom. One of the room's two windows was wide open. A stiff breeze periodically rushed in to push a curtain away from the wall. Piggybacking on the wind, the smell of smoke, most likely from a neighbor's fireplace, raced up his nostrils.

From inside the room, he noticed the door's trim, near the lock, was missing large chunks of wood. And the door itself had splintered; the lockset having almost fallen out.

He turned toward the center of the room and saw a pair of black panties, a black bra, and sheer black stockings laying haphazardly on a neatly made bed. Beneath the wide-open window, a woman's three-inch-high, pointy-heeled red pump rested under a side table along with everything that had presumably been on the table at one point—alarm clock, lamp, ceramic coaster, as well as a few trinkets.

Lockhart stuck his head out the window to see footprints in the snow at the base of the window, leading toward the garage on his left. Even though the footprints had been disturbed by blowing snow, it was still clear that the left print had been made by a high-heeled shoe while the right one was in the shape of a human foot.

After verifying the shoe under the table was the 'right' half of a pair, he made a pass around the bedroom, looking for clues. And under the bed, he found an important one, an employee identification badge for a bank in Adder. Standing, he read what was on the badge. *Tricia Stefanik. Customer Service Representative.* Holding the rectangular object 'up and down,' he stared at the picture at the top, memorizing the thirty-something's features—long, straight blonde hair, narrow face, dark eyebrows, pointy chin—before tucking the badge into a jacket pocket.

•••

Two Minutes Later...

Outside, Lockhart stood next to the garage, his eyes following the tracks from the bedroom window to a second set of tire tracks next to McCord's SUV. Walking the 'second set,' he noticed shoe prints in the snow, bigger prints that would indicate a man's shoe, perhaps a work boot of sorts. The prints came from the back door, joined up with the tire tracks, then stopped ten feet away from the SUV's rear bumper before turning toward the back door again.

Lockhart inspected the area. Moments later, he squinted at something shiny in the grooves left by the second vehicle's tire treads. He stooped and picked up a twenty-two long rifle case, the same caliber that had made the hole in McCord's forehead.

Continuing down the tire tracks, the lawman

stopped behind his Jeep and stared at the pavement. The road crews had not yet been by. For the next few minutes, he surveyed the compacted snow, searching for evidence that might prove his theory. Using his boot to push aside snow, he kept looking back at McCord's house, estimating trajectories.

The toe of his Ariat came down on something hard.

He squatted and carefully cleared away the snow. Two beats later, he picked up a round shard of glass. Poking around the area, he uncovered several more pieces before he stood and turned toward the driveway, contemplating his theory. Moments later, he hauled out his cell phone.

"Hey, Wade," said Piper. "How did it go with McCord?"

Lockhart envisioned the man's corpse. "Dead end." He then added more pertinent details before finishing with, "Get someone out here to process the scene."

"I'll have Bristol send out the nearest deputy."

"Call me if he finds anything useful."

"Are you on your way back?"

"I need to make a stop first," replied the sheriff.

"Where?" asked Piper.

He plucked the ID badge from his pocket and eyeballed it. "I'm thinking of opening a bank account."

CHAPTER 4
ADDER BANK & TRUST

Adder Bank & Trust took up the first floor of a two-story building on a street corner in busy, downtown Adder. And with the lunch-hour rush in full swing, people dressed in winter garb—coats, hats, gloves, boots—traversed the sidewalks. Hustling to pay a bill, pick up a prescription, meet up with friends for lunch at a nearby restaurant, or whatever, everyone had something to do, and most had only an hour to get it done.

On congested streets, with their exhaust pipes sending smoke clouds high into the air, cars and trucks stopped at streetlights, turned left or right, or quickly swerved into one of the few open parking spaces along the busiest stretch in Adder.

Having parked his Jeep two blocks up the street, Lockhart now strode toward the bank's front doors. From over his right shoulder, he heard a nearly constant groaning. He knew the sound. It was the sound of a car's starter engaging with the vehicle's flywheel. But crank after crank, instead of the motor starting, it only groaned and moaned.

Lockhart peeked through the bank's windows, on his left, to see a small lobby with carpeted floors, overhead lighting, and a row of wooden padded chairs lining the street-facing windows.

The motor ground again.

Opposite the bank's windows, there was a six-foot-high wall/countertop with five customer service stations cut into the wall. The middle three stations were staffed and had customers standing at them.

Reaching for the front doors, hearing the poor engine making another attempt at pleasing its owner, Lockhart backed away from the doors to see where the noise was coming from.

Five parked cars down the street, a young teen was behind the wheel of a burgundy, older model two-door car.

Lockhart could see the kid glancing around, as those passing by him peered through the windows but kept on going. He could just imagine the youngster's embarrassment, as he sat there hoping that this time, the car would start. The sheriff glimpsed the bank lobby then headed for the stranded motorist. *Hope doesn't usually get cars started.*

Coming upon a late 70s Buick Century with a slanting 'fastback' rear design, Lockhart knocked on the driver's window.

Inside, a young man in his late teens leaned forward to roll down his window.

     RECKONING

"Afternoon," said Lockhart, a smile gracing his features for less than a second. "Sheriff Lockhart. Big Sky County." He flashed his badge.

Sporting short, jet-black straight hair, dark eyes, and medium-to-dark skin, the teen matched the lawman's greeting, both in intensity and duration. "Hey," he replied. "Am I in trouble?"

Lockhart shook his head. "Not with me, but I'd say you are with," he motioned toward the hood.

"Yeah," sighed the teenager, "this thing's done this before...when it's cold outside. It's only ever happened in the morning, though, after it's been sitting all night. I've never had it happen in the middle of the day like this."

"Pop the hood for me." Lockhart strolled to the front bumper.

The hood popped up a couple inches.

He snaked fingers underneath and raised the hood to its full height.

The driver got out and hunched over the engine compartment.

"What's your name, son?" asked Lockhart while he unscrewed a wingnut on the Buick's air cleaner.

"Diego."

With the wingnut off, Lockhart lifted the air cleaner to expose the carburetor. "Just as I thought."

"What?" asked the kid, his eyebrows coming together.

"Well, Diego, your choke plate is completely closed, so your carb's not getting any air." Lockhart saw confusion written all over Diego's face. And since he didn't have time to explain all the parts of a carburetor, he motioned toward the passenger compartment. "Go start it for me."

Diego got into the car.

Lockhart pushed open the choke plate.

Seconds later, the motor was running rough as the vehicle visibly shook.

He worked the throttle lever a few times then let the engine rev until the idle smoothed out.

Diego joined his 'mechanic.' "How'd you do that, man—I mean—*Sheriff*?"

Lockhart gave him a two-minute crash course on carburetors, highlighting the choke plate and how the bimetal coil spring responded to hot and cold temperatures, before he assembled everything and closed the hood.

"Thanks, Sheriff. I really appreciate it."

"No trouble at all." Lockhart wiped his dirty hands on his white handkerchief while stepping onto the curb. "Remember, go easy on that accelerator on cold mornings."

The kid smiled back. "I will."

"And if this happens again, use your—"

"A *glove* to wedge open the choke until it starts," finished Diego.

Lockhart flashed him an upturned thumb, "Good man," then headed for the bank.

. . .

Ten Minutes Later...

With two elderly women behind him, Lockhart waited near a floor sign that read, 'WAIT HERE FOR NEXT AVAILABLE CUSTOMER SERVICE REP.'

A man at the second station walked away and headed for the front door.

A blonde woman leaned across the countertop and smiled at Lockhart. "I can help you right here, sir."

Stepping aside, he motioned toward the teller while facing the woman behind him. "Go ahead, Ma'am."

"Are you sure?" she replied.

"Positive."

"Well, thank you, young man." The gray-haired woman ambled toward the second station, relying on her metal cane for assistance.

The third station, the middle one, became available.

Lockhart strode straight ahead while studying the blonde-haired woman behind the counter. She had straight hair, a thin face, and a pointy chin.

"Good aft—" the woman turned away to cover a yawn before coming back to him. "I'm so sorry. How can I help you, sir?"

He noted her heavy eyes, drawn features, and overall lethargy. She seemed primed for a nap. Plus, there had been a hint of leftover alcohol in the air after her yawn.

He spied her nameplate on the counter. "Rough night, Tricia?"

"Oh," Tricia Stefanik closed her eyes and half shook her head before glimpsing him again, "you wouldn't believe me if I told you."

"You never know." He drew back his jacket to expose his sheriff credentials before placing her ID badge on the counter. "I just might." Lockhart had never seen the color in someone's cheeks drain so fast. He was prepping himself to lunge across the counter to grab her and keep her from falling if she passed out.

Tricia hung her head while gripping the counter for a few seconds.

"Is there somewhere private we can talk?" asked Lockhart while picking up her badge again.

Raising her head, she glanced behind her. "There's a meeting room back there." She faced him. "Can I check out first? I don't want my till all messed up."

He nodded. "Just make sure you don't leave my sight."

• • •

Ten Minutes Later...

The meeting room had beige carpeting, overhead lighting, and black vertical blinds covering a window that faced the area behind the tellers. A monitor, computer keyboard, and a round container for pens sat on a dark cherry, closed-front office desk. One padded office chair sat behind the desk while two padded straight-back chairs were in front.

Not wanting to surrender his authority, Lockhart had directed Tricia toward the straight-back on the left while he had claimed the other. This way, he could read her entire body language as she answered his questions.

Wearing black slacks, black flats, and a black, open-front sweater over a white blouse, Tricia sat with her legs crossed at the knee. She alternated between crossing her arms over her belly and holding her head in her hands as she spoke.

"It was around two or three in the morning, and—"

"*This* morning?" interjected Lockhart.

She nodded.

Lockhart scribbled in his notepad. "Go on."

"Pete and I were fooling around in the bedroom. We had just gotten to his place after closing down the bar. We hadn't really done anything yet when the doorbell rang. I told him to ignore it, but he couldn't let it go. Said it was only going to *distract* him." She gave the sheriff a sheepish look. "I'm sure you know how it is."

"And then what happened?"

"Pete answered the door, and a second later, I heard a heavy thud. I got up and left the bedroom while calling out his name." Tricia closed her eyes. "That's when I saw him."

"Who?"

"The guy with the gun, standing over Pete. I saw him, and he saw me. That's when I locked myself in the bedroom." Tricia cupped her right elbow and covered her face. "I knew Pete was dead. He had a hole in his head, and there was this line of red running over his forehead." Drawing her hand down her face, "I knew he was dead," she repeated, slamming shut her eyes, her face contorting into something ugly.

Lockhart watched her wipe a tear away from her right cheek. "Were you and Pete intimate? Were you dating?"

Tricia laid her hands on her lap, her right one on top of her gold wedding band and diamond ring. "No." a beat. "We met last night."

"At this bar you mentioned?"

She nodded.

He asked the name of the bar, she answered, and he wrote it in the notepad. "Then what happened...after you locked yourself in the bedroom?"

Tricia filled her lungs, looked away, then sighed. "This guy began beating on the door. I knew it was only a matter of time before the cheap thing would give out. So, I threw on my clothes, stuffed what I could into my purse, and crawled out the window."

"Did you have a cell phone on you?"

She nodded.

"Why didn't you call the police?"

"Because I thought I was going to die. I only had

seconds before he kicked in that door, and the police would have been *minutes* away."

Lockhart couldn't disagree with her. "So, you crawled out the window. Then what?"

"I ran to my car and got the hell out of there." Tricia squinted at her questioner. "Did you know that crazy bastard chased after me?"

Lockhart waited.

"I backed out onto the street. But before I could drive away, he started shooting at me. Shot out the window on my side of the car. Pieces of glass flew everywhere."

Lockhart reviewed his notes, her statement. Everything she had said lined up with what his theory had been back at McCord's house. The twenty-two-caliber case lying in the snow, the glass shards he had found in the road, the squiggly tire tracks on the driveway—indicative of someone backing up in a hurry—they all matched with Tricia Stefanik's statement of events. "Where did you go then?"

"I was too upset to drive home, so I crashed at a girlfriend's house. I tried getting some sleep, but I couldn't. I just laid there in bed, my mind seeing that guy, seeing Pete." Tricia rubbed her forehead then let out another long sigh. "So, I got up, showered," she pinched her sweater then let go of it, "borrowed some clothes from Brandi and came to work."

Lockhart wrote 'Brandi' in his notepad. "I'll need a last name, address, and contact information for this

Brandi.”

Tricia nodded. “Of course.”

“If you saw him again, do you think you could identify the man who shot Mr. McCord?”

“I don’t know. It was dark, and he had a baseball hat on, pulled down low.”

“How tall was he? What was his build?”

She half closed one eye. “He wasn’t a big guy. But he wasn’t skinny either.”

“Height?” prompted Lockhart.

“Maybe not quite six feet tall.”

“What was he wearing?”

“Light-colored pants. They would’ve probably been a khaki color in the daylight, I think.”

Lockhart wrote.

“His hat was a dark color—plain, no writing or emblems on it. And he had on some shorter length black jacket. I think it was leather. And it had,” she touched her collarbones, “white up near his neck—like the collar was like a white fur or something. You know, like an insulated jacket?”

Lockhart took down everything she said. “Anything else you can remember, Ms. Stefanik?”

Tricia put both feet on the floor, leaned forward and held her face in her hands. “I don’t know. I’m not sure. My mind is kind of scrambled, and I haven’t gotten any sleep.”

He closed his notepad. “Where is your husband right

now?"

Taken aback, she casually covered her wedding rings again.

He raised a hand. "I'm not here to shine a light on marital indiscretions. My only concern is for your safety."

She frowned. "My safety? What does that have to do with a robbery?" She motioned toward his notepad. "You're going to arrest that guy, aren't you? Put him away?"

"I don't think you understand the situation, Ms. Stefanik. Robbers don't shoot people in the forehead with 22-caliber pistols then chase after those who run away from the scene. Robbers want to rob when no one is home. They want to get in, then get out with whatever they've stolen."

"What are you saying, Sheriff? Was Pete *intentionally* murdered?" Tricia put a flat hand to her chest. "Is someone now coming after me, to kill *me*?"

He could see she was getting worked up again. "All good questions, ones I intend to get answers to. Now, where is your husband?"

"He's," she scratched a furrowed eyebrow, "he's out of town—for work. Won't be home until," she shook her head, "until next week sometime."

Lockhart nodded to himself. *Probably for the better.* "Ms. Stefanik, whoever killed Mr. McCord," *he's a professional*, thought Lockhart, "he might see you as someone who could identify him to the police." Once again, he saw the color drain from her face. "So, I'd like to offer you protection. I can assign a deputy to be with you wherever you go."

"What about while I'm at home?"

"You shouldn't go home."

"Why?"

"It's possible the killer may know—or find out—who you are and where you live. I'd feel much better if you'd let me set you up at the hotel in Wyatt. It's close to the Sheriff's Office."

Tricia thought for a few moments. "Can I still go to work?"

"As I said, a deputy will be with you wherever you need to go."

She took another few moments before bobbing her eyebrows once and sighing. "If you think that's best, okay."

He stood. "Carry on with your day here. And tell no one of this conversation or what happened. Understood?"

She nodded then rose from her chair.

"I'll have a deputy here within the hour. He'll be posted outside at all times."

Tricia looked up at the sheriff, her features softening a bit. "Thank you, Sheriff." She then held out her hands, palms down, and watched them tremble before rubbing them together. "I'm scared."

"Maybe you can ask your boss for the rest of the day off. Then you can get some sleep once you're settled into your hotel room."

Nodding, she laid her right hand on her hip while reaching up to massage her temples with a thumb and middle finger. "Yeah. I can ask him."

"I'll be here until my deputy arrives. After that, if you need me, or remember anything else from this morning, let the deputy know. He'll get in touch with me."

Tricia nodded. "Okay."

"Thank you for your time." Lockhart donned his Resistol hat and opened the door.

"Sheriff?"

He faced her, noticing deep lines on her forehead.

"You *are* going to catch this guy, right?" she asked.

He gave her a brief smile. "Don't worry, Ms. Stefanik. Nothing's going to happen to you."

1:27 P.M.
WYATT, MONTANA
SHERIFF'S OFFICE

Tricia had gotten permission from her boss to leave early from work. So, Lockhart had driven her to her home and waited while she had packed a suitcase with clothing for a few days. After driving her to Wyatt, he handed her off to his deputy, instructing the deputy to get her settled into a hotel room then stand guard outside the hotel.

Now, having exited his office, Lockhart stopped at Piper's desk.

Reclining in her chair, her crossed ankles resting on the corner of her desk, the undersheriff was busy rubbing her eyes with the heels of her hands.

Lockhart laid hands on his hips. "Find anything in Jace's reports?"

Startled, Piper swung her feet off her desk and stood. "Nothing yet." She wriggled her hips while hoisting her gun belt higher up her waist. "I've gone back another month, but I've found nothing unusual."

He nodded.

"Oh, and I checked into Tricia Stefanik's girlfriend, Brandi."

"And?"

"She confirms that Tricia showed up at her place around three-thirty this morning and was there until Tricia left for work." Piper cocked her head. "So, you think we have a hitman roaming the streets of Big Sky?" Lockhart had updated Piper while Tricia had been packing a suitcase.

"Evidence points that way."

"And here I thought I'd left all those big-city crimes behind me when I got out of New York to come to sleepy Montana." She poked her chin at him. "How does this tie in with Bronson?"

Breathing in, he wrinkled the right half of his face while staring out the window next to her desk. "My hunch is that whoever took out the initial contract on Jace is now getting rid of everyone involved."

"Just so I understand, we're operating on the assumption that Bronson's telling the truth and that there *was* a conspiracy to kill Jace."

He faced her. "Don't you think it's quite the coincidence that Bronson tells me about McCord, and I find McCord's body an hour later?"

"Yeah, but only you, me, and Bristol knew you were going to see Bronson. Besides, McCord was killed twelve hours ago, long before you went to see Bronson."

"Doesn't mean something wasn't already in the works to kill McCord."

She folded her arms across her chest. "How deep do

you think this goes?"

"Depends on how many players are involved."

"So, more bodies could drop?"

Lockhart nodded then lifted a finger toward her. "Send a deputy over to the hotel to show Tricia Stefanik some mugshots of our more hardened criminals. It's a long shot, but maybe she'll recognize one of them as our hitman."

Piper bent over her desk and scribbled onto a three-by-three notepad. "Will do."

He slipped into his office and closed the door partway.

. . .

Minutes Later...

Tina Walters passed through the saloon doors and stopped at Bristol's desk. "Hi, Bristol."

"Well, hello, Tina. What brings you by?"

"I saw the sheriff earlier today, and I told him I'd stop by later to drop off something for him. Is he busy?"

"He's not with anyone, so," Bristol swung a hand toward Lockhart's office, "go on back."

"Thanks." Tina strolled toward a seated Piper.

"Hey, Tina," said Piper, her eyes on her computer screen.

"Hi." The newcomer stopped short of Lockhart's open office door. "Is he busy?"

"Wade?" called out Piper. "Tina's here."

"Send her in," replied Lockhart.

"Hey," Piper turned toward Tina, "did you get that box of stuff I left for you?"

The younger woman bent at the knees while arching her back to roll her eyes at the ceiling. "I am *so* sorry. Yes, I did. I should've texted you."

Piper flipped a wrist. "No worries. Did they fit?"

Tina recalled the clothing items in the box. "I tried them all on, and they fit perfectly. Thank you." She frowned at the other woman. "But they looked brand new, though. Some even had the store tags on them."

Inwardly wincing at her carelessness, Piper came clean. "That's because they are. Brand new. From the store."

Tina cocked her head. "Wait. You said you had a friend who was my size and had some clothes she wanted to get rid of."

Piper gave her a mischievous grin. "I *do* have a friend who's your size. And I'm pretty sure at some point she's probably said something like that to me."

The truth dawning on her, Tina shook her head at Piper. "You didn't have to do that."

"No, I didn't." Piper leaned back in her chair and folded arms across her chest. "But that's what friends do for each other."

Tina closed her eyes, her cheeks flushing. "Are all you people here so dang sweet and kind?" She flapped her hands toward herself. "Come here."

Piper stood.

The two embraced.

Tina pulled away a second later but held on to her friend's hands. "Thank you. I mean it. Most of my clothes were," her former profession flashed across her mind, "well, they weren't quite appropriate for my new life. Let's leave it at that." She leveled a finger at Piper. "And I'm going to pay you back, too."

"Go ahead and try. I dare you." Piper sold her humor with a wink and a smile. "Those are gifts. You never repay gifts."

Tina hugged her again. "Thanks, Piper."

"You're very welcome."

Tina walked into Lockhart's office while knocking twice on his half-open door. "Knock, knock."

• • •

Lockhart sat at his desk, holding his desk phone to his face. "Thank you, Judge Thomas. I appreciate you considering this matter. As I said, I would prefer the gory details of my son's murder not be made public."

Tina stood at a distance, glancing around the sheriff's office, not wanting to appear to be eavesdropping.

"I'll wait for your decision before submitting my official report." Lockhart listened. "Thank you again, sir. And good day to you, too." He 'hung up' the phone then stood while beckoning his visitor. "Come on in."

She complied, meeting him at the front of his desk. "Here." She held out a wad of cash. "This is what I was talking about this morning. I got a late Christmas bonus from work and wanted to pass it on to you."

He eyed the folded bills and estimated she had a few hundred dollars.

"I know it's only a fraction of what I owe you, but I wanted to show you that I haven't forgotten."

"Listen." He pushed her hand, and the money, back toward her. "I want you to keep that. In fact, as of this moment, your debt to me is wiped clean."

Shaking her head, she looked him in the eye. "No. I can't do that. Here." She thrust out the cash. "Take this."

He intertwined his forearms and perched on the edge of his desk. "I know you're not making much money, and I don't want you worrying about paying me back." He dipped his forehead toward the money. "I can see you're determined to make good on what you owe me. Your noble intentions are good enough for me." He gestured toward the money again. "Save that for a rainy day. Life being what it is, you're probably going to have something unexpected pop up. And when it does, you'll have the funds to take care of it."

"But I owe you a lot," she rubbed a watering eye, "both financially *and* for all your help in setting me up here."

"Seeing you turn your life around, and knowing I

    RECKONING

played a minor role in that, is worth more than a couple thousand dollars."

Turning away from him, she brought her left hand to her mouth while laying her right fist, bills inside, on her hip. A second later, she sniffed. "First Piper, and now," her voice cracked, "and now you. I don't deserve this."

Noticing her shoulders shuddering, Lockhart snagged a tissue from a square box on his desk, drew up on her left, and held the tissue in front of her. "Everyone deserves a second chance."

Tina accepted the offering. "Yeah, well, I come from a family, a *religion* where if you," she wavered, "if you mess up, you're an outcast among your own people." She ran the tissue over her nose. "But here, you people know my past, my mistakes, and you don't turn away. Instead, you go out of your way to *help* me." She huffed. "I think I'm finally starting to understand what Jesus meant when he said, love one another as *I* have loved you."

"We're all on our own unique journey to God, I guess." Lockhart looked out the window, his mind going back to what he had said to her earlier that day, out on the sidewalk: *God be praised.* Twice in one day, he had acknowledged God. That wasn't him. His wife Cheryl had always been the religious one, going to church, volunteering, helping at various charitable events. He had simply gone along so that he could spend time with her. He had considered himself a barnacle that had attached itself to her ship's hull. Lockhart inwardly chuckled.

Once, he had said that same thing to her, 'I'm just a barnacle attached to a hull,' and she had looked at him sideways, joking a tick later, 'I'm not sure how I feel about being called a *hull.*'

"Anyway," continued Tina, "sorry for the preaching."

"That's quite all right."

She regarded him for a moment, then threw her arms around his midsection.

He hugged her back, his chest absorbing her gentle sobs.

Fifteen seconds later, she retreated to dry her eyes, cheeks, and nose. "I don't know what to say. I've never," a beat, "everyone here has been so," she sniffed again and continued to wipe away tears. "I'm sorry. I'm a mess."

"No. You're just a normal person with people who care about you. Nothing *messy* about that."

Tina composed herself then held up the money. "Are you sure?"

Lockhart raised his hands in surrender. "I'm sure."

Hugging him again, "Thank you so much, Sheriff," she finished off with a harder squeeze before backing away.

"You know, you *can* call me Wade."

She eyeballed the bills, "No," before stuffing them into a jean pocket, her mind tallying everything he had done for her, "no, I really can't." She met his gaze. "I respect you way too much."

"People can use first names and still respect each

other.”

She held a shrug while tipping her head to the side. “Maybe someday.”

He nodded. “Okay then.”

“Well, I better get back to work. I told my boss I’d only be gone twenty minutes.” Tina smiled. “Bye, Sheriff.”

Raising a hand, he watched her leave his office.

Treadway's Bar & Casino was located one block west of Main Street in Dunbar. The structure looked like three large metal storage buildings joined at different angles. With a flat roof, sides painted a dull gray, two exterior windows, and a gravel parking lot, its signage's paint peeling, it wasn't much to behold on the outside. But people here didn't care about the exterior. They came for the spirited atmosphere and that Old West feeling.

Inside, Treadways was truly a holdover from days gone by. From the front door, a boot-scuffed, long wooden bar sat off to the right. Green-felted circular wooden tables, with wooden straight-back chairs scattered around them, filled the rest of the interior. Two wagon wheel chandeliers hung from chains overhead. Black-and-white pictures of wagon trains, horses, and men and women dressed in old-time western clothing adorned the walls. There was even a black piano in the back-left corner. The only thing missing from the scene were the swinging saloon doors.

With semi-loud country music playing from speakers

mounted in the bar's four corners up by the ceiling, Lockhart observed the dozen or so people sitting at the tables. They were talking and laughing while tossing back beers or hard liquor. Most were dressed in Western garb, while one looked to have been a truck driver, which would explain the 18-wheeler he had seen outside.

Carrying his Henry Big Boy by the receiver, down by his right thigh, Lockhart approached the middle of the bar, catching the eye of a man in his late forties in the reflection of a fifteen-foot-wide mirror on the wall behind the bar, above liquor bottles resting on a wide shelf.

Sporting dark eyes, thin lips, a pointed chin, and black hair on his round head, the five-nine Chance Treadway finished pouring a beer, delivered it to a table, then returned to stand across from Lockhart. "Wade."

"Chance."

The owner spied the sheriff's rifle. "Must you always bring that in here? My clientele gets a little nervous when they see it."

Lockhart grinned. "Only those who *should* be nervous."

Chance mimicked the man's gesture.

Lockhart and Chance were old friends. They had met in boot camp and quickly hit it off. While the former had made a career out of the Army, the latter had left the service for riches and fame on Wall Street. And he had succeeded. But the money hadn't brought him happiness.

Moving to Montana and opening this bar, however, had a major, positive impact on his state of well-being. Treadways wasn't much, but it was Chance's pride and joy. And the money he had made on Wall Street had been enough to give him a comfortable life here.

"Did you get the check from the last time I was in here?" asked Lockhart.

"Yes, I did. And I do not wish to have a repeat of that day."

Having had too much to drink, a biker had picked a fight with the sheriff. And using the butt of his rifle, the sheriff had loosened a few of the man's teeth before hauling him off to jail. During the scuffle, Lockhart had shattered a mug on the biker's skull before breaking a couple bar stools.

Lockhart leaned the 44 Magnum against the bar. "I'm only here for information."

"Funny you should say that. Because you were only here for information on your last visit as well."

The men shared another lighthearted exchange.

Chance pulled the towel off his shoulder and began wiping the bar. "What can I do for you, Sheriff?"

"I'm hoping you might know who I'd talk to if I wanted to take out a contract on someone."

Chance stopped wiping, his eyes shifting toward his friend. "You mean a *hit* job?"

Lockhart nodded.

"First of all, what makes you think I would possess

such information, and second," a pulse, "who are you looking to have killed?"

Lockhart placed the toe of his boot on the bar's seven-inch ledge down by his foot. "It's for a case." He looked down for a moment before returning to Chance, his face somber. "I have reason to believe Jace's murder was no traffic stop gone bad. I think someone wanted him dead."

The bartender threw the towel over his shoulder and leaned on his palms, his own facial expression now matching that of his friend's. "I'm very sorry to hear that, Wade."

"So, if you know of anything that can help, I'd sure appreciate it."

His chest heaving, Chance turned away, his brain searching for answers for his long-time ally. "Offhand, I do not know of any such person; however," he drew a hand over his mouth then laid it back on the bar, "I've been slowly amassing an unofficial list of contacts. A few of them might be able to get you the information you seek."

"Unofficial list of contacts?" echoed Lockhart.

"Bartenders are like psychologists. Only we're less expensive and not," a twinkle manifested in Chance's eye, "bound by patient confidentiality."

Lockhart lifted a corner of his mouth, half chuckled, then picked up his rifle. "Remind me to watch what I say around you."

Chance returned a half grin then turned serious. "I'll make some calls and get back to you."

"Thanks," replied Lockhart, before making his way toward the door.

•••

Outside, Lockhart climbed into his Jeep and shut the door while fumbling around in his coat pocket. Rocking right, he retrieved his mobile, spied the incoming number, then answered. "Hello there."

"Hey, where are you right now?"

"Dunbar."

"You up for an early dinner? I missed lunch, and I'm starving."

Lockhart had been feeling hunger pangs for the last hour. "You read my mind. Although, I must warn you. I'm waiting on a call and might have to skip out early."

"I'll take however much time God gives me with you."

He smiled. "What did you have in mind?" His features turned sour when he heard his caller's restaurant of choice. "But they don't allow dogs in there."

"Why *would* they? It's for *people*."

He started the Grand Wagoneer and put it in 'Drive.' "Meet me at the Sheriff's Office in an hour. I know a better place."

CHAPTER 7
CHARLENE'S PLACE

Eight miles east of Wyatt, the census-designated place (CDP) of Crawley had a total area of four-point-five square miles and a population of fifty-two people. The CDP was mostly farmland with a couple cattle ranches on the southern side. But in the center of Crawley, south of a railroad line and across from the post office, stood Charlene's Place, a restaurant known for serving some of the best food in Big Sky County, including hamburgers, steaks, and cheesesteak sandwiches.

Charlene's had a low brick wall in front of vertical wooden boards for its exterior frontage. Two wide windows were to the right of a glass door, while wood shingles adorned a short and wide, mansard-style roof design.

Inside, the restaurant featured an open floor plan with several dining areas, each partitioned off on three-and-a-half sides by five-foot-tall walls, leaving only a five-foot-wide section for visitors and wait staff to come and go. This layout made it so no one could see anyone else in the restaurant.

Seated facing the gap in the wall, the 'doorway,' Lockhart spied the woman on his left, admiring her blue eyes. She had a longer face that exhibited gentle curves at the jawline and cheekbones. With an off-center part, her medium-length, wavy blonde hair fell just below her collarbone, overlapping with her black, long-sleeved turtleneck sweater.

39-year-old Sierra Courtright pivoted her head to take in the framed pictures on the wall on her twelve o'clock, Lockhart's two o'clock. "That's," she lifted a finger, "a show dog right there; *American* line, I'm pretty sure."

Lockhart cranked his head to see her pointing at a photo, the photo of a black-and-tan German Shepherd from a left-side viewpoint. The dog was standing on green grass on a sunny day.

"You can tell by how the back hips," she motioned with a flat hand, "slope down so much." She half smiled. "Beautiful animal."

He came back to her. "You really know your German Shepherds."

Sierra gave the other pictures, all of them GSDs, another glance. "When I adopted Ranger, I made it my mission to get to know everything I could about the breed. I was blown away by what I learned." With her right hand, she reached down and patted her dog Ranger's head. "They're intelligent, loyal, fearless animals that will give their lives for their owners." She transitioned to stroking his muscular neck. "Isn't that right, boy?"

A 90-pound male GSD, standing 26-inches at the shoulder, Ranger laid on a three-foot-square, three-inch-thick bed in the corner between Lockhart and Sierra. Most of the dog's face, his ears, the back of his neck, his back, sides, and tail sported black fur. His shoulders, hindquarters, legs, chest, and underbelly were a reddish, deep mahogany color, making him a black-and-red German Shepherd.

Ranger closed his eyes and tilted his head as his owner's fingers tickled the base of his ears.

"All right," a mid-fortyish woman with short, bottle-black hair, wearing blue jeans and a white dress shirt, sleeves rolled up to her elbows, entered the personal dining area.

Ranger raised his head and focused on the woman.

Holding a pencil and pad of paper, "What can I—" she stopped in her tracks when she saw Lockhart. "Well, looky who it is. Mister Wade Lockhart."

He smiled. "Hello Betsy."

The woman huffed. "How've you been, stranger? Why, I haven't seen you in here in years."

"It hasn't been that long," countered Lockhart.

"Well, you certainly don't come as often as you did when Cheryl was alive."

Lockhart shot a nervous glance at Sierra, who was smiling at their chipper server.

"You and her used to stop in several times a month. In fact," she went to tiptoes to peek over the wall, toward another dining area, "if I'm not mistaken, you'd always ask for the Siberian Husky booth." Each dining area was named after a specific breed of dog, and all the pictures in that booth were of the same kind of dog.

"Yeah," Lockhart shifted in his chair, giving Sierra another quick peek before eyeing their server, "she always loved her huskies."

A beaming Betsy took another moment to regard her male guest. "It's good to see you, Wade. You're looking like your old self again."

"Thanks."

"So." Staring at Lockhart, Betsy hooked a thumb toward Sierra. "Are you going to introduce us?"

He sat taller. "Right. Betsy, this is Sierra. Sierra, Betsy. She's an old friend from high school."

Betsy frowned at him. "Did you have to say *old*? You know I'm a year younger than you."

He chuckled.

She smiled at Sierra while extending her right hand. "It's nice to meet you."

The women shook hands.

"It's nice to meet you as well."

"And," Betsy eyed Ranger, "who's the one staring at me back there? I don't think he's blinked once since I came in."

Sierra patted her dog. "This is Ranger. Don't worry,

though. He won't bite you. He likes women over men."

"Then how did," Betsy motioned toward Lockhart, "this guy manage to get so close?"

"Oh," Sierra regarded the man on her right, "Ranger knows a good guy when he sees one."

"Amen to that, sister. Wade is definitely one of the good ones." Betsy stood poised with pencil and paper in hand. "What can I get you folks?"

Sierra raised her brows at Lockhart. "I'll have whatever you recommend."

"Sure. Put all the pressure on me." Without ever having opened it, he handed his menu to Betsy. "Two cheesesteak sandwiches with thick wedge fries."

Donning a partial smirk, the server claimed his and Sierra's menu. "Two of your *usuals* then."

Lockhart squirmed at the emphasis on 'usuals.'

"And to drink?"

"Water for me," replied Sierra.

"Same," said Lockhart.

"All right. I'll be back with your waters."

When their server had left, Lockhart cleared his throat then gave Sierra an awkward, fleeting look.

She noticed. "What is it?"

"I-I'm sorry for all that."

Frowning for a split-second, she half grinned in the next moment. "For what? She's delightful."

"No. That's not what I meant. Betsy's great. It's just that," he wavered, "well, I'm sorry she kept bringing up my," he took another moment, "my wife. I know how women—women *and* men—can get when past loves get mentioned."

Sierra leaned toward him and put her right hand on his left. "Wade, we both have past loves. Yours passed away. Mine decided he didn't want to be with me anymore. Heck," she tipped her head toward the doorway, "the way Betsy fawns over you, you two might have had a thing going back in the day."

"No." He shook his head. "No. We were never—"

"I'm joking," said Sierra.

He relaxed.

"And even if you two *had* been something, I wouldn't have cared. Like I've said before, however much time God gives me on this earth, I'm not going to waste it dwelling on the past." She took his hand in both of hers. "I'm not a jealous woman. I'm not competing with memories. You loved your wife, and I once loved my ex-husband. But you and I are here *now*, together. So, let's just appreciate the moment, see where God takes us."

For the next few seconds, he enjoyed the sparkle in her eyes. From somewhere behind him, a soft light was playing across her face. His gaze took him to her lips. Listing her way, his stare never leaving hers, he gave her a long kiss, his lips barely touching hers.

"Okay, here's your wat—uh-oh," said Betsy as she slipped into the space.

The couple parted.

"Sorry." She set the tall glasses on the table and smiled. "Happens all the time. We servers here are sneaky that way."

Lockhart and Sierra exchanged glances.

"Good news. You beat the dinner rush, so the cook is working on your orders as we speak. Should only be another ten minutes."

"Thank you, Betsy," said Sierra.

"You're welcome."

"Thanks," said Lockhart.

The server left again.

Still reveling in the kiss—a kiss that was somehow deeply passionate yet innocent at the same time—a blushing Sierra took a drink of water, wishing she could have dipped her fingers into the cold liquid and cooled her warming chest.

"Listen," Lockhart leaned back in his chair, "I have a surprise for you."

"Ooh, I love surprises. It's a good one, right?"

"*I* believe it is, but you'll have to be the one who decides that."

She recalled how she had deferred to him on what to have for dinner. "*Now* who's the one under pressure?"

"Yesterday, I met with the board and put a proposal before them."

Not expecting this to be work related, Sierra cocked her head at him.

"Ever since you and Ranger helped Piper and me

track down Davis Bronson, I've been mulling over an idea."

With her curiosity mounting by the second, Sierra inclined toward him.

"Earlier today, I got a call from a board member, and—if you want it," he paused, "you and Ranger are approved to become part of the Big Sky Sheriff's Office."

Taken off guard, Sierra straightened her back.

"I know you said you left law enforcement behind you, but I also remember you saying that law enforcement never really leaves *you*. So, if you accept, then Big Sky will have its very own K-9 unit."

Sierra took another sip of water while staring straight ahead.

"The position would be on an as needed basis, but I did get the board to approve a guaranteed salary based on ten hours a week. But if you end up working *more* in one year, which I don't see happening, then the County would start paying you by the hour for however many hours you're over."

"So," Sierra's brows wrinkled, "even if I end up only working," she wavered, "say fifty hours in a year, I'd still get paid my entire annual salary?"

"That's right."

"Why would they approve that? It's cheaper to hire me at an hourly rate right from the start."

Lockhart nodded. "True. And a couple board members made that same argument; however, I informed them you work for yourself, taking jobs as they come in. So, having you on the payroll, as an official Big Sky employee, would bump us up to the top of your list whenever we needed your help." He looked at her. "I hope I didn't overstep my bounds there."

She smiled and squeezed his hand. "I'd bump you up any day."

"Okay, so," not sure if she was referring to the job offer or something else, he half grinned, waited a few seconds, then asked, "so what do you say?"

She spied Ranger. "What do you think, boy? Want to go to work?"

His ears picking up the last part of her question, Ranger stood and stared at his handler, his tail wagging.

"Oops. That was too close to one of his commands." She patted him. "Ranger, break."

The GSD relaxed.

"Down."

The dog turned around once and laid down on the mat.

"Good boy." Sierra faced Lockhart.

He arched his brows. "Well? Shall I place an order for your business cards?"

She smiled. "Ranger and I accept. We'd love to be your dedicated K-9 unit."

• • •

One Hour Later…

Lockhart and Sierra had finished dinner fifteen minutes ago and had been chatting for the last quarter-hour when he felt his phone vibrating. He pulled out the flip phone and eyed the exterior screen. "This is the call I've been waiting for." He opened the device and put it to his left cheek. "Lockhart."

In his ear, Chance Treadway's voice: "Wade, I have a name for you."

Lockhart scrambled to get his pen and pad ready.

"One that may have information on the services you're looking to procure. Kellen Riley."

Lockhart wrote. "Do you know where I can find him?"

"I have his home address as well as an establishment he frequents quite regularly."

The sheriff scribbled, taking down the addresses.

"And," continued Chance, "do not ask me where this information came from. Just know that I believe it to be true."

Lockhart recalled his earlier conversation with Chance, the part where Chance said bartenders are like psychologists. "I think you have more psychologist in you than you're willing to admit."

Two seconds passed.

"I am now hanging up on you, Wade."

Chance kept his promise, and Lockhart let out a quick snicker before stowing his mobile and facing

Sierra. "I need to go."

She fluttered her open hands, pretending to shoo him away. "Go. I understand. After we stop for gas, Ranger and I are heading back to your place."

He stood, took out his wallet, and left a more-than-generous tip for Betsy before plucking a couple more twenties and snatching the bill.

"I can get that," said Sierra. "After all, *I* was the one who asked *you* to dinner."

"Nope. Lockhart dates don't pay. Personal motto."

"That can get to be an expensive motto."

Lockhart stared across the room. "When I was in junior high, there was this girl I was smitten with. At the time, I didn't have much money, but I did have the courage to ask her out." He paused, reminiscing.

"And?" prodded Sierra.

"Unfortunately, she said yes."

"Unfortunately?"

He spied her. "Not much money, remember?"

"Ah. Right."

He glanced down at the bills he held. "Anyway, when I told my father about what I had gotten myself into, he gave me a twenty along with some advice." Lockhart regarded Sierra. "Lockhart dates don't pay, son. We take care of our women."

She smiled. "Well, thank you."

"Not sure when I'll be home, so don't feel like you have to wait up for me."

Sierra's heart skipped a beat. She had been staying at his house, in the guest bedroom, whenever she came to Big Sky. Lockhart had even purchased and set up a dog bed next to her bed. Even though their relationship was in its infant stage, it was heartwarming to hear him say 'home' and 'you' in the same sentence. "I'm sure Ranger will let me know when you're home."

He helped her with her coat then donned his own.

"Again, thanks for dinner. It was great. I really like this place."

Lockhart headed for the doorway. "Best in Big Sky."

"Ranger, heel," she said.

The dog stood and drew up on her left side as the trio left the booth.

"I'm curious," said Sierra. "How did the date go—from junior high, I mean?"

Lockhart shook his head once. "Terrible. Oil and water." He raised a finger. "But I still picked up the check, though."

Not finding Kellen Riley at his home, Lockhart had then traveled to the establishment Chance had said the man frequents regularly, Peaks & Valleys, an adult entertainment club located south of the interstate and five miles west of Buck. The 50x30-foot metal, A-framed building—with a covered entrance—sat on a stretch of snowy terrain. Off in the distance, in every direction, mountain peaks rose from the valley.

With a dozen or so vehicles parked haphazardly on the dirt parking lot/driveway, tall security lights shining downward, Lockhart got out of his Grand Wagoneer and strolled toward Peaks & Valleys' red front door at the far-right end of the structure. Once inside, closing the door behind him, he stood in a six-by-eight-foot antechamber. Vertical beads hung from an archway straight ahead. Knifing through the beads, he stepped into the main room, into an 'alternate reality' of sorts, and found himself facing a stage the size of his office.

The stage sat in the center of the room and was surrounded by bar stools. Two shiny poles, twelve feet apart from each other, went from the stage to the ceiling.

Two-person tables lined the walls on his three o'clock and nine o'clock. A bar area was at the far end, on his two o'clock, while several doorways were against the wall on his ten and eleven o'clock. The doorways had curtains; all were drawn. Above the doorways, signs read 'PEAKS & VALLEYS EXCLUSIVE ROOM.' Each room had a different-colored, soft glow emanating from around the edges of its curtain.

On the stage, a woman pranced around one of the poles in a bra, panties, and black platform heels, periodically squatting down or dropping to her knees, so men could slip dollar bills into her skimpy lingerie.

Speakers pounded out a rhythmic tune that really wasn't a song so much as it was a collection of different notes. The atmosphere was dark, with the stage being lit by crisscrossing beams from overhead lamps. Ambient light showed patrons hooting and hollering while holding up money. Others simply talked with whoever they were with. Everyone had a drink in his hand.

Sporting a smile, a twenty-something, long-haired brunette dressed in a black midriff corset top, pink thong, and patent-leather chaps, chaps that were actually high-heeled boots that attached to a wide belt around the woman's waist, approached the newcomer. "Welcome to Peaks & Valleys, sir. Would you like a table, or will you be sitting at the stage?"

"Neither. I'm looking for a man named Kellen Riley. Have you seen him?"

She took a barely perceptible half-step backward, shot a look over her right shoulder, then came back to him. "I don't want any trouble."

Lockhart saw in her eyes the look of a puppy that had made the mistake of trying to cuddle up to its drunken owner one too many times. "What makes you think you're in trouble?"

She pasted a fake smile on her face. "Can I seat you at a table, or do you prefer the stage?"

Beyond her right shoulder, he noticed two wide-bodied men 'standing guard' outside the far-right Exclusive Room, the one with a red glow coming from around its curtain. He spied the young woman. "I'll take a table, Miss."

She escorted him to a table on his ten o'clock, near the door, then asked, "Can I get you something to drink?"

Pulling a twenty-dollar-bill from his wallet and laying it on the table, he then drew back the right half of his jacket.

Her eyes went from him to his badge before bulging a bit when they settled on him again.

"I promise. You're not in any trouble. But I do need to know if Kellen Riley is in here tonight."

She fidgeted in place.

"Don't point. Don't look in that direction. Just tell me one thing. Is he in the *red* room?"

She took a breath, closed her eyes, then nodded quickly.

"Thank you." He slid the 'twenty' her way. "Bring me whatever drink you want and go on about your evening as if we never had this conversation." He tapped the note. "Keep whatever's left over."

The server picked up the money and headed toward the bar area, returning two minutes later with a beer.

He nodded and smiled at her then pretended to ogle the dancing woman. While his peripheral vision took in the 'Red' room, his brain sized up the two men on either side of the archway. *All muscle and no real-world experience.*

Two minutes later, he stood and ambled away from his table, making a right-ninety at the stage.

Something flashed across his vision, going from right to left.

After glancing at the floor on his left, to see a woman's bra, he pivoted his head to the right to see the now half-naked dancer smiling at him while trying to reel him in with her slowly curling right index finger.

He kept going, stopping when he got to the 'Red' room to eyeball two men wearing baseball hats cocked off to one side, high school varsity jackets of sorts, sweatpants, and white tennis shoes. "Gentlemen." He exposed his badge. "I'm looking for Kellen Riley."

"He busy right now," said a black man on the sheriff's eleven o'clock.

"Yeah," added the other man, "he *gettin' busy* all right."

'Eleven O'clock' and 'One O'clock' shared a laugh.

"This is official business," said Lockhart.

"He should be done in," Eleven eyed a gold watch that probably cost about as much as the sheriff made in half a year, "fifteen minutes."

Lockhart whipped off a single headshake. "Can't wait that long." He stepped forward.

Both men closed ranks to block the archway.

"I said," the six-three Eleven stared down at Lockhart, "he busy. *Fifteen* minutes."

"And *I* said," thrusting up-turned hands forward, his left one closing around Eleven's testicles, while his right one squeezed One's 'package,' Lockhart got a deep hold, "I can't wait that long."

The henchmen's eyes grew huge as each man went to tip toes and sucked in a big breath.

"Walk with me." Lockhart pivoted counterclockwise.

Eleven and One shuffled to their right.

"That's it. Baby steps." When he had ushered the human obstacles out of his way, he tightened his grip, leaned in close, and said, "Don't follow." Lockhart let go, pushed aside a curtain, and entered the Exclusive Room.

Bending in half, Eleven and One gasped while holding on to the stage for support.

· · ·

Inside the Exclusive Room, a room not much bigger than a full sheet of plywood, a blonde woman—wearing a red G-string, bra, stockings, and heels—was straddling a shirtless, seated man in his thirties, grinding away on his lap, as he cupped the woman's butt cheeks.

"Kellen Riley?" said Lockhart.

The woman whipped her head toward the intrusion.

The man launched into an obscenity-laced verbal assault.

Lockhart displayed his badge, "Sheriff Lockhart," then eyed the woman. "Give us a moment, will you, Miss?"

She backed out of the chair and left the room.

"Are you Kellen Riley?"

Baldheaded, and sporting tattoos of every kind up and down muscular arms, the man kept shooting glances at the closed curtain.

Lockhart noticed. "They're nursing stomach aches at the moment."

The man gave the curtain a last look, huffed, then shook his head in disgust. "What do I," he raised his voice, "pay you guys for, anyway?"

"Are you Kellen Riley?"

"Yeah, I'm Kellen."

"I need to ask you some quest—"

The curtain parted.

Lockhart drew his Ruger and aimed it at Eleven's face.

The man froze, his eyes crossing to gape at the gun's muzzle, an inch from his nose.

"What did I say?"

Eleven retreated.

Lockhart holstered his Redhawk.

"You mother," Riley cursed, "are useless. Useless!"

"Do you know a man named Pete McCord?"

"Petey? What's he gotten himself into?"

"So, you know him?" prompted Lockhart.

"Yeah, I know him. We've done business before."

"Like arranging contract killings on sheriff's deputies?" Lockhart saw a flash of recognition in the man's eyes.

"Is that what he told you?" said Riley. "He's lying. I ain't never killed anyone. I run a legit business. I have an auto repair shop in town. I don't kill people. I fix their rides."

"I never said you killed anyone. I asked if you *arrange* for people to be killed."

"Listen. Whatever that damn fool Petey tells you, it's a lie, okay? He only brings me cars. Broken-down cars that need fixing. I buy them, fix them, then sell them for a profit." Riley flung an arm toward the sheriff. "Ask him yourself."

Lockhart opened his phone, found a picture he had taken, then showed Riley the screen. "Wish I could."

Riley scowled at the image. "Is that—"

"Pete McCord? Yes."

"Is he—"

"Dead? Very much so. The work of an assassin."

Lockhart stowed his mobile.

Riley cocked his head at the lawman.

"Why, you ask?" Lockhart glimpsed various photos on the wall, photos of attractive women in various stages of undress. "Good question, Mr. Riley." He leaned back against the wall and stared at the other man. "One I'm sure you can answer."

With his forearms resting on the lounge chair's armrests, Riley flipped his palms toward the ceiling. "How should I know? What Petey did was Petey's business."

Lockhart gave the man a long, hard glare. "You're not fully comprehending the gravity of this situation, sir. I know you were involved in murdering one of my deputies."

Riley shook his head. "No. That ain't—"

"Shut up!"

Riley faced the sheriff.

"While I can't prove it *yet*, I can almost guarantee that you hired McCord to find someone to kill my deputy."

Riley crossed his legs, ankle on knee, and looked toward the curtain.

"Now, whoever killed McCord is looking to tie up," Lockhart jabbed a fore finger toward Riley, "loose ends. So, whether you want to admit it or not, your life is in danger."

Riley scoffed. "Ain't nobody dumb enough to come at

me."

Lockhart hooked a thumb toward the wall on his right. "Because those pansies outside will protect you?" He huffed. "You'll be dead by the end of the week."

Riley's cheeks turned red while his fingers gripped the armrests. "Nobody come at me, because they *know* what I'll do to them, *personally*." He made a fist and thumped his chest one time. "I settle my *own* accounts, Sheriff."

"I don't care about your debtors. I want information on your lenders, those above you; specifically, the people who hired you to arrange a hit on my deputy. Tell me, and I can take you into protective custody, keep you safe from this assassin."

Riley sneered at the man across from him. "You ain't got nothing on me. If you had, I'd already be in cuffs. So, with that," he examined his fingernails, "if you done, then I need to get back to business." His smile grew wider as he leaned forward, scooped up a red lace garter, and twirled it around his finger while looking up at the sheriff. "If you know what I mean."

Lockhart squinted at the man for a few seconds then pushed away from the wall. "Have it your way. But if you're interested in living," exiting the room, he said over his shoulder, "call me."

7:11 P.M.

In the guest room at Lockhart's house, lying in bed and propped against the headboard, with three fluffy pillows strategically placed under her back and head, a table lamp on her four o'clock, Sierra turned a page in her Bible and continued reading Jesus' words from John's Gospel. *The hour is coming, and is now here, when true worshippers will worship the Father in Spirit and truth.*

On her three o'clock, Ranger lay curled up in a ball on the dog bed Lockhart had bought him. His droopy eyes popped open when his owner turned the page. In fact, they popped open whenever his owner made even the tiniest of motions.

Sierra yawned. Dinner had been great, both the food and the conversation. Okay, more so the conversation. She flipped back a page and held the paper between her fingers. *Believe me, woman, the hour is coming when you will worship the Father neither on this mountain nor in Jerusalem.* While she and Lockhart had gone out before, none of those dates had come close to the intimacy the two had shared today. After closing her eyes, forcing them open, then blinking several times, she let the sheet fall to the left before reading the ending of the first verse again...*true worshippers will worship the Father in Spirit and truth.* She frowned. *Spirit and truth.* Feeling another wave of fatigue coming over her, she clenched her teeth together, but couldn't hold back another yawn.

Reading the Bible for meaning—that is, trying to internalize passages, hear God's Voice—could be tough when you were well-rested and focused on taking in His Word; however, when you were tired, and feeling like a schoolgirl who had just gone out on her first date with that cute boy from math class...well, taking in God's Word could be downright impossible.

Sierra closed the Bible and ran the zipper around the dark-brown leather case protecting the 'Good Book.' She sighed at the cover's front, at the religious image of a cross debossed into the leather. *Forgive me, Lord. The spirit is willing, but the flesh is weak.* After laying the Bible on the nightstand and rearranging her pillows, she turned off the lamp before plopping onto her right side, facing Ranger. "Good night, Range."

Two minutes later, she went to her back before rolling onto her left side. She situated the pillows again and closed her eyes. Thirty seconds later, she opened them, her mind buzzing, replaying different parts of her time with Lockhart. He had really opened up to her, more than at any other time in their budding relationship. It was pure joy to sit and listen to him talk about things he enjoyed as well as the things he didn't enjoy.

Ranger took a breath and exhaled loudly.

Hearing him, Sierra smiled at how Lockhart had chosen this afternoon's restaurant, precisely because they allowed dogs. He liked Ranger, and Ranger had accepted him into his 'family of two.' Now a family of three. Her smile broadened at the thought of her and Lockhart one day becoming an actual family. She closed her eyes and nestled her left cheek deeper into the pillow. *Don't let go of the rope too soon, Sierra.*

From behind her, a low, deep growl grew louder.

Sierra opened her eyes at the sound. She had heard it many times at her home in Wyoming. Usually, it meant some animal had wandered too close to the home. Male GSDs were particularly protective of 'their' property. She shut her eyes again. *Whatever's out there will move on.*

Ranger got up and trotted toward the bedroom door, his ears up, his head cocking one way and then the other.

Watching him, she noticed his hackles were up.

He growled. This one, however, went longer than usual, then built to a crescendo before Ranger barked once, leaped onto the bed, and spun to face the doorway, his tail in Sierra's face.

She went to her left elbow. "What's going on, boy? What's got you so riled up?" She patted his hind quarters. "Lots of strange noises in this new place?"

His tail curling upward, he lowered his head and frame, posturing as if he were preparing to pounce.

Sierra rolled right, retrieved the Smith & Wesson Shield Plus she had put in the nightstand, then reversed course. She pulled on the gun's slide a hair, to verify a round was in the chamber, then threw off the covers and got out of bed. Wearing a gray long-sleeved, oversized sweatshirt that fell below her butt, and a pair of cable knitted thigh-high winter stockings, also gray, she stood near the footboard, her right sock having slid down to her knee.

Turning her head to the left, while tucking her tousled, long hair behind her right ear, she strained to listen. Out of the corner of her eye, she saw Ranger still poised to attack whatever came through the open bedroom door.

A minute later, she faced the doorway, debating whether she should go see what was up. Usually, homeowners had the advantage when navigating their home in the dark. But this wasn't her home.

Thirty seconds passed.

With her Smith & Wesson in her right hand, she crept toward the door.

Letting out two high-pitched barks, the German Shepherd leaped from the bed and pressed the right side of his body against her knees, his herding instincts kicking in.

"Sit," she whispered.

The dog obeyed.

She showed him her left palm, "Stay," then plodded

ahead. Even though the animal had been trained to charge into buildings and locate criminals, she was uncomfortable with sending him to do what she herself wouldn't do. Call her crazy, but Ranger meant too much to her to be used like a tool, like some hammer or crowbar. Besides, if she really were in danger, she knew the 'stay' command wouldn't keep him from coming to her aid.

The GSD lowered his head and leaned toward her before sitting tall again and puffing out his chest, his front paws dancing in place while he whimpered.

I know, boy. Sierra gripped her nine-millimeter with both hands and poked her head out into the hallway. *I'll be careful.*

• • •

Behind the wheel of his Jeep, having left the strip club ten minutes ago, Lockhart navigated the highway, his thoughts focused on the pavement beyond his headlights, focused on what his next move would be. *Do I even have a next move?* Proof, evidence, witnesses, he didn't have any of those things. And without them, he was forced to wait, wait for a break.

His phone vibrated.

He saw it was Piper and flipped open the device. "Lockha—"

"Dispatch just got a call, a woman reporting a

prowler."

"Okay. Get a deputy—"

"Wade, the woman gave the operator *your* address."

He scowled. "Sierra?"

"Not sure. The line went dead. I'm on my way there now."

Lockhart slammed shut his phone, activated the siren and light bar, then stepped on the accelerator.

• • •

Twenty Minutes Later...

Lockhart overshot his own driveway, and the Grand Wagoneer bounced over a mound of snow before fishtailing left. He corrected his mistake and got the vehicle pointed in the right direction before jamming his foot onto the brake pedal.

The Jeep skidded to a halt over packed snow.

He scrambled out of the SUV, drew his Ruger, and bolted for the front door of his home, slipping twice on powdery snow, as he bypassed Piper's truck.

Piper met him on the front porch, her open hands facing him. "It's okay, Wade. She's fine."

He pulled up and caught his breath, his revolver down by his right leg.

"I arrived ten minutes ago and let myself in with the key you gave me a few years back. After I identified myself to Sierra, I found her holed up in the bedroom with Ranger."

Lockhart went around his undersheriff and burst into the living room to find Sierra on the sofa, Ranger on her left.

Seeing him, she jumped up and met him at a coffee table.

The two embraced.

His vise-like grip caused her sweatshirt to rise up over her butt and expose a sliver of short, loose-fitting black shorts. "Are you okay?"

"A little shaken, but I'm okay."

Stepping inside, Piper closed the front door behind her. "I searched the house and the property. No burglars."

The couple parted.

"I feel so stupid," said Sierra, while regarding Piper. "I'm so sorry for dragging you out here like this. I—"

"No," replied Piper. "You did the right thing."

"Having been one, I know how it is for cops. I know the adrenaline rush when you get those calls. You were probably speeding the whole way here."

Piper gave the embarrassed woman a cheery smile. "Are you kidding me? Speeding's the best part."

Sierra let a half smile come and go. "I'm still sorry. I thought about searching the house but turned back at the last minute...since I don't know the layout that well."

"No," said Lockhart. "Piper's right. Better to," he glimpsed the Smith & Wesson on the coffee table, "get your gun, call 9-1-1, and wait for backup. You made the right decision."

"And then," Sierra gestured toward her phone on the coffee table, "my cell dropped the call to 9-1-1 halfway through."

He holstered his Redhawk while facing Piper on his right. "Did your search turn up anything? Were there signs of anyone sneaking around outside?"

"I found footprints in the snow at the front of the house and along the west side. Looks like they lead to where a car had been parked. Judging by the tire marks, the car was parked there recently."

"Show me." Lockhart turned away from Sierra then quickly pivoted back. "Are you okay?"

She waved him off. "I'm good. Go. Find out who was here." She sat on the couch and put her left arm around Ranger.

· · ·

Outside, with Piper hovering over his right shoulder, Lockhart held his cell phone down by one of the least disturbed tracks in the snow, near the northwest corner of his house.

Piper squinted at the image of a print left behind in the snow, a print of a man's boot. "They're darn near identical." With the temperature dropping quickly, she stood tall, shoved hands into coat pockets, and hunched her shoulders.

He got to his feet. "But it's not definitive proof our assassin was here. Any burglar, any *man* could buy the same set of boots."

"And you're sure," she pointed at his phone, "those prints are from the guy who killed Pete McCord?"

"The only other tracks at the man's house were mine, Tricia Stefanik's, and ones that I later matched with a pair of men's dress shoes I found at the back door of McCord's place."

"If that's true, and our assassin *was* here, then *why* was he here? You're a sheriff, for crying out loud. Was he planning to kill you, too?" She shook her head. "That makes no sense."

Lockhart slid his phone into his jacket pocket, blew into cupped hands, then rubbed them together, his mind running through scenarios. Finally, he settled on one that unnerved him. "He was waiting outside Tricia Stefanik's house."

Piper observed him. "What?"

"Our killer must've discovered where Tricia lived and was waiting for her to come home. If she hadn't gone to her friend's place, she—along with her friend—probably would've been murdered, too. Then, when I drove her home to pack a bag, the killer must've still been waiting."

"He saw you with her and what," interjected Piper, "followed you back to Wyatt?"

Lockhart's blood ran cold as he faced his second in command. "Where he then watched me hand her over to—"

"The deputy," interrupted Piper. First on the draw, she had her phone out and was dialing the deputy who was on duty, the deputy who was supposed to be standing guard outside Tricia Stefanik's hotel. "Come on. Come on. Pick up."

...

Five Minutes Later...

Piper disconnected the call to the deputy and stood staring at the device.

"Piper?" said Lockhart.

She gaped at her phone.

"Talk to me. What is it?"

The woman closed her eyes and drove three fingers into her forehead. "Tricia Stefanik is dead. The deputy found her in her hotel room with a bullet hole in her head."

Lockhart ground his teeth together while looking away. "Just like McCord."

She nodded. "A twenty-two; right between her eyes." A pulse. "The deputy swears he saw everyone who entered the hotel lobby. Everyone was either staying there or were inquiring about staying there. Nobody out of the ordinary got by him."

"Listen, Piper. The hotel must have security cameras. I know you've had a long day, too, but I need you to review them. I'd go myself, but," he motioned toward the house, "but I—"

"No, no. Of course. Someone needs to be here with Sierra. And that's you. I get it. I'll head to the hotel."

"Thanks. And watch your back. This guy might think Tricia ID'd him and is now taking out anyone who crossed paths with her. That's most likely why he came to my house. He figured she told me what he looked like, and he was going to kill me before I exposed him."

Piper nodded. "I'll be safe."

"Call me if you get something, okay?"

"Will do."

CHAPTER 10
COZY NOOK

After Lockhart had seen Piper to her truck, and given her a final admonition to stay sharp, he had then backed his Jeep up to the house before spending the next hour with Sierra in what he called his home's 'cozy nook.' This cozy nook was partitioned off from the rest of the living room by a three-foot-high spindled wooden handrail that jutted out from the front wall and made a right-ninety to join up with the west wall. Access to this sunken area came in the form of a gap in the handrail. Amenities included dark-red shag carpeting, a loveseat, two padded straight-back chairs, two small side tables, and a gas fireplace in the northwest corner.

Now, with only a couple low-wattage nightlights on throughout the home—to guard against anyone outside from getting a sight picture on them—Lockhart and Sierra sat on the loveseat, he on her right. Watching the flames dance in the fireplace, each person held a cup of tea.

Ranger was laying in front of the heat source, facing his owner, his head on the floor between his paws.

Sierra sat on her right hip, her heels up against her

butt, with a multi-colored crocheted blanket pulled up to her chin, her hands wrapped around her cup. A second later, her eyes drooped. Feeling warm, she freed her left leg and laid it on the blanket.

Lockhart sipped his tea while staring at her exposed gray boot sock. "I'm curious."

Her right shoulder pressing on the cushion behind her, she pushed a lock of hair away from her face while observing him.

He lifted a finger. "What's with the tall socks? Why not just wear sweatpants or," he paused, "or something else that covers your legs?"

She spied the legwear in question. "Whenever I wear sweatpants to bed, the material rubs against the sheets, twisting every time I change positions. I end up feeling like I'm all tied up and stuck to the bed."

Internally commiserating with her, Lockhart nodded. Long pants did the same thing to him at night; however, as a man, 'other things' got twisted by the long pants every time he changed sleeping positions.

"I like to sleep in shorts and a t-shirt," continued Sierra, "or a *sweatshirt* when it's cold out. But I'm usually chilled when I first go to bed." She sipped her beverage. "Years ago, I was so tired one night that I just left my ankle socks on. And I discovered I was more comfortable. So, the next night, I found a pair of knee-high socks, and was even warmer."

He lifted a corner of his mouth. "So, the socks got

higher and higher with each passing night?"

She half smiled. "Sort of. Right around that time, I saw this woman wearing knee boots one day. She had on a pair of tall socks underneath them. They came up over her knee and looked just so cute on her. That's when I thought to myself," Sierra touched a fore finger to her lips, "Hm. I wonder." She reached down and pulled the slouching sock further up her thigh. "So, I bought a pair online and fell in love the first night I wore them to bed. Now I have several sets in different colors."

Lockhart half squinted at her. "But you're not in bed right now."

She bobbed her head from side to side. "Even around the house, I prefer shorts to pants. But my legs get cold. So, I wear these." She huffed. "If I'm anywhere *near* being active, though, these things slide down. I'm pulling them back up every five or six steps. But for lounging, on a cold night, they're warm and super comfy." She shrugged. "Tradeoffs, I guess." Regarding him with a side eye, she ran a palm over the cable knit part of the sock. "Why? Do I look silly in them?"

He shook his head. "No. You look fine. They match your sweater, and they," he wavered, "they," before nodding, "they look good. You look nice in them."

Sierra smiled. "Well, thank you."

Lockhart inspected her sweatshirt. Before she had crawled under the blanket, he had noticed how long and baggy the garment had been on her. He thought she had purchased it a few sizes bigger to have room to move. Now, however, getting an up-close look at the clothing, he noticed the front of the collar, right below her chin, was frayed. The same thing happened to his shirts after years of rubbing against his beard stubble.

"What is it?" Sierra held a flat hand to her chest. "Is there something on me?"

"No," he replied before reaching behind her, examining the apparel's tag, and seeing it was the same brand as his sweatshirts. "Is," his brows came together, "is this mine?"

Her cheeks darkened a bit as she ran a hand over her upper chest. "Yeah, I forgot to pack a sleeping shirt when I left home. I saw this," she pointed toward the other part of the living room, "on the couch over there and thought I'd wear it to bed. I hope you don't mind. I'll wash it before I go home."

"Don't worry about it." Lifting the blanket to see the sweatshirt paired with her socks, as well as the thin strip of white skin in between, he puckered his lips and nodded. "You wear it well. Looks better on you than it does on me." He let go of the blanket and went back to staring at the fire.

Sierra dipped her chin and took a slow sip of her tea, using the act to disguise her smile, as a warm sensation flooded her body and soul. *Two compliments in one night.*

Ten minutes later, Sierra forced her eyes open before letting out a yawn. "I think my adrenaline rush has worn off. I'm beat." She pushed the blanket aside, stretched out her legs, then placed her feet on the floor. "I should probably let Ranger out once more before going to bed."

"I can do that. I'm still in street clothes."

"Are you sure? It's cold out there."

"I'm tough," he replied before eyeing Ranger. "Will he listen to me?"

Sierra regarded her dog then faced her questioner. "I think so. You're part of his family now."

"Ranger, come," said Lockhart.

The dog raised his head then trotted to him.

"Good boy." He patted the dog's neck while tossing Sierra a look. "Did I do that right?"

She nodded. "Positive reinforcement is always good. As long as you're happy, *he's* happy."

"Wanna go outside?" said Lockhart. "Go pee?"

Ranger wagged his tail.

"Come on, buddy." Lockhart stood, donned his leather jacket, then headed for the front door while throwing Sierra another look. "Here's hoping I don't lose your dog."

"You won't lose him," she said with a snicker.

He opened the door, and Ranger went outside, Lockhart following while closing the door behind him.

Sierra hurried to the front window and pushed aside the curtain with one finger, her ears picking up Lockhart's muted voice.

Outside, the sheriff roughhoused with Ranger then

flung his arms toward the darkness. "Go on. Go pee."

Ranger stared at Lockhart, his tail wagging.

"Trust me, man. Eight hours is a long time to hold it."

The dog jumped up, wrapped his front legs around Lockhart's waist, and barked twice.

A standing Lockhart clutched Ranger's neck and shoulders and tossed him back and forth, as the animal 'fought' back, taking playful bites of the man's forearms.

Sierra watched them tussle in the snow. Lockhart was good for Ranger. The dog's original handler had been a big man, bigger than Lockhart. And she had been told that the GSD loved the rough stuff and that he and his handler would mix it up regularly, both getting in a good workout. Sure, Ranger would play ball and fetch a stick; however, what he craved was the physical contact, the opportunity to exercise his powerful muscles. Sierra had tried playing games like tug of war. But with her being only twenty pounds heavier than the 90-pound dog, tug of war quickly became 'toss the rag doll' with *her* being the rag doll. With Lockhart, though, Ranger had strong competition, and he was loving the raw challenge. Plus, she could see Lockhart was having fun, too. She lifted a corner of her mouth. *Maybe even more than Ranger.*

After watching them for a few more minutes, Sierra wandered toward the guest bedroom, her heart feeling as big as the smile on her face.

•••

Fifteen Minutes Later...

The quiet of the house, the surrounding darkness, her mind envisioning Ranger on the bed, his hackles up, ready to attack whoever had been sneaking around the home earlier; all those things had come rushing to greet Sierra as soon as her head hat hit the pillow, and she had closed her eyes.

She had felt safe sitting with Lockhart by the fire. *Nobody can get to me if he's around*, she had told herself. It was a silly notion, but silly notions can become real if one believes in them. Just like some regard faith in an unseen God as ridiculous. But to those with faith, God is real and living. She rolled onto her left side and stared at the open doorway, her right hand crushing the pillow she lay on. *You're a cop, Sierra. Toughen up, will you?*

Whether or not she admitted it, her past abduction and assault had done a number on her confidence. She had put on a brave face for her coworkers back in New York, telling them she was doing 'fine.' But unbeknownst to her, deep inside, where bone and muscle met soul and spirit—where only God's Word could penetrate—she knew she had been wounded, wounded at her core. And tonight's events had reminded her that the healing process was not yet complete.

The sound of the front door opening and closing made its way upstairs. Seconds later, with his toenails clicking against the hardwood floors in the hallway, Ranger burst into the second-floor bedroom and hopped onto the bed.

Sierra let him sniff her face and hair—so he knew she was okay—while a waft of the cold temps outside, coming from his damp coat, rushed up her nostrils. Fortunately, he had shaken off the snow somewhere between here and the outdoors. She then directed him toward his place on the floor.

He jumped off the bed and laid down in his own bed.

A minute later, she sensed a presence before seeing a silhouette in the doorway.

"Are you awake?" whispered Lockhart.

"Yup," she replied. "Can't really sleep."

"Thought you might want to know that he never went pee. He wanted to horse around in the snow, so we played for a bit and came back inside."

"That's all right. He'll wake me if he needs to go."

"All right then." Lockhart grabbed the doorknob. "Good night."

Sierra shoved her upper body away from the mattress to lean on her outstretched left arm. "Wade?"

"Yes?"

"Will you," she faltered, biting her lower lip while building up the courage to finish her sentence.

Lockhart caught the distress in her voice. "Are you okay?"

"No, not exactly. Would you," she swallowed, "would you mind staying with me—just until I fall asleep? I'm not trying to," *seduce you*, she thought, "get you to do something you're not comfortable with. Honest, I'm not. It's just that I'm still a bit," she inwardly chided herself over her lack of courage, "I'm still unnerved over what happened tonight, and I'd feel better if you were close by."

Lockhart glanced over his shoulder, toward his bedroom down the hall, then came back to her before lowering his head to stare at his boots. He hadn't been with a woman since Cheryl had died. Sure, this wasn't a sexual invitation from Sierra, but in the last five years, he had never even *looked* at another woman in that way. He rubbed a hand down his face, unsure if he was ready for this. In the next moment, he thought, *Ready for this? If I'm not ready to simply stay with a woman until she falls asleep,* he filled his lungs and exhaled, *then I'll never be ready to actually BE with another woman.*

In the dim lighting from the hallway nightlight, Sierra could make out his facial features, strained features that spoke more than any words could. "I'm sorry." She waved him off. "I'm being a sissy. I shouldn't have asked. I'll be okay." Sierra fixed the covers then plopped onto her left side before fluffing her pillow. In the next instant, she spied him. "It's okay, really. I'll be fine. Ranger's right here."

Lockhart gave his bedroom door another glance then ambled toward Sierra to sit on the edge of the bed, facing the doorway. After pulling off his Ariat boots and setting them off to the side, he pivoted on his butt and stretched out on her left.

Privately smiling, "Thank you," she said, her voice a hair above a whisper.

He rolled her way, kissed her on the forehead, then rolled back before crossing his arms over his chest and getting comfortable. "Sleep well."

She slid her legs up and down a few times, nuzzled under the covers, then let her body sink into the mattress. *I will NOW.*

Sierra woke to the smell of bacon in the air, but no man in her bed. She rolled onto her back and stretched her arms above her head. After glancing toward Ranger's bed, and not seeing him there, she looked toward the doorway to see that the door was closed.

Throwing off the covers, she took a moment to scratch her skull before running fingers through her hair, straightening it where locks were twisted. Following a second yawn, she rummaged around under the covers for her socks. Most nights, she usually ended up kicking them off when she got too warm. Finding the tall stockings, she pulled them up to the middle of her slender thighs then left the bedroom.

Halfway down the hallway, mindful of her short black shorts, she pushed Lockhart's sweatshirt further down under her butt while tracking the smell, and sound, of frying bacon.

Lockhart's voice: "What? You want some of this?"

She heard a low whimper.

"Sorry. You've had your breakfast."

At the end of the hall, Sierra slid her right hand along the smooth wooden banister and quietly took the first two steps before stopping to see Lockhart sliding a frying pan back and forth on a stove-top burner. His back was to her. He was dressed and looked to have showered and shaved as well. She bent at the knees and leaned left to spy Ranger sitting near the stove and looking up at the chef. He had those same pleading eyes he used with her whenever he had wanted a morsel of people food.

"Don't look at me like that." Lockhart held his hands out to his sides, a pair of tongs in his right hand. "I don't make the rules."

Smiling, Sierra covered her mouth to suppress a laugh.

"You'll have to take that up with your owner."

Unable to hold back her amusement, she let a barely perceptible snicker slip between her fingers.

"Besides, I'm pretty sure you can't have—"

Ranger whipped his head toward the sound before his ears went back, and his tail began wagging, as he ran toward Sierra.

Lockhart turned around to see her first stooping, then dropping onto her butt when her dog greeted her on the stairs. "Good morning," he said while returning to his task. "He's already eaten and done his business."

"Good mor—" being pushed by her enthusiastic GSD, Sierra rocked backward. "Good morning." Laughing, with her knees bent, and Ranger climbing onto her lap, his tongue lashing out to give her a 'kiss,' she rotated her head left and right, trying to dodge his advances. She hugged his neck and patted her dog's shoulder while his tail waved back and forth. "You must've really—" Ranger got in a lick across her chin, and she laughed some more, "really missed me, huh?"

"Of course, I missed you," replied Lockhart while doling out bacon slices. Scrambled eggs were on two nearby plates and waiting for the strips to arrive.

Sierra smiled at the back of his head, "Very funny," then got to her feet before pushing down her top and pulling up her socks. "Has he been good for you?" She descended the rest of the steps and entered the kitchen.

"He's been my *shadow* this morning. Followed me wherever I went. He even found his way into the bathroom while I was showering. I must not have closed the door all the way. Startled me when I threw back the curtain."

She chuckled. "Yeah, he's done that to me a few times, too. He can be sneaky when he wants to be." She pressed her right hip into the counter, patting Ranger while watching Lockhart handle the cookware. "What time did you get up?"

"When," Lockhart gestured toward the pet, "*he* decided my face would make a good salt lick. Speaking of which," he held up a shaker while eyeing Sierra.

She crinkled her nose and shook her head. "No

thanks."

"I hope you're hungry." He salted his eggs then transferred the plates to the table where utensils, napkins, and drinking glasses were setting. "What do you want to drink...juice, milk, water?"

From off a paper-towel-covered serving plate, Sierra plucked a crispy section of bacon and broke off a chunk between her teeth. "Milk sounds good."

"Have a seat, and I'll get you some."

She sat, covered as much of her butt with the sweatshirt as possible, then crossed her legs under the table. "The bacon is great."

"Yeah," he filled her cup with milk, "hard to mess that up," then returned the container to the fridge.

Probably hoping his charms would work better on her, Ranger sat on Sierra's right, staring up at the food she held.

Lockhart got a glass of water and claimed the spot on her two o'clock, Ranger between them.

"So, he woke you up, huh?" She picked up her fork and dug into the eggs. "He usually does that to *me*."

"Well," Lockhart picked up on the hint of a bruised ego in her tone, "maybe he knew you needed the extra sleep."

She smiled, partly because of his rationale, but mostly because she was simply enjoying breakfast with the man who had stayed with her, comforted her, when she had needed comforting. "Just wondering," she bit into a bacon strip, "but how long did you stay with me last night?"

"Until," Lockhart shoveled eggs into his mouth then pointed with his fork, "*he* woke me up."

Sierra started to go for her eggs but stopped to stare at him. "Wait a minute." Her mind was piecing together a timeline. "You said Ranger woke you up this morning?"

"Uh-huh."

"So, he went into your bedroom?"

"No. He came around to my side of the bed...*your* bed."

"So," a pulse, "you stayed with me the whole night?" she asked, tingles racing up and down her spine.

Lockhart nodded before taking a drink of water.

Sierra lowered her head to stare at the near edge of her plate, her heart thumping as she bottled-up a smile. *He stayed all night long.*

"Listen." He wiped his mouth with a napkin. "I'm going to take another run at Kellen Riley this morning."

Having been briefed on everything pertaining to this case, Sierra nodded, relieved for the change in topic, so she could gather her composure.

"I'm hoping a good night's sleep has changed his mind, and he's now ready to help me." Lockhart shrugged. "Then again, he may be beyond reason. I don't know. Anyway," he faced her, "I was thinking I could drop you off at a friend's place on the way there."

She frowned at him. "What do you mean?"

"After last night, I'm not comfortable leaving you here all by yourself. I still don't know if that guy came here looking for me, you, or," Lockhart paused, "or whoever he came across."

Sierra laid her fork down, wiped her mouth, then placed the napkin next to the fork. "I was afraid this was going to happen."

He spied her. "Afraid *what* was going to happen?"

"I should have never asked you to stay with me."

"What are you talking about?"

"Look, I appreciate what you did and all. It was very sweet. But I don't want you seeing me as weak and feeble, or as someone who needs taking care of." Sierra heard the hypocrisy in her words. Yes, she wanted someone to take care of her. Who didn't? She just didn't want that someone to see her as a person unable to fend for herself.

Lockhart set his utensils down and pivoted in his chair to see her squarely. "Who said anything about you being weak and feeble? I'm looking at this from a tactical standpoint. With more people around you, helping you, you'll have a better chance at protecting yourself should someone come after you."

She cocked her head at him, surprised at where he was coming from. "So, this isn't you making decisions for me...like I'm a helpless two-year-old?"

"Of course not. You're a grown, adult woman. You can take care of yourself."

"And what if I said no to you dropping me off?"

He tilted his head and sighed. "I wouldn't like it, but I'd certainly respect your wishes." He looked at her. "I just want you to be safe, because that's what friends, or in our case," he ran forefingers back and forth between her and him, "*boyfriends and girlfriends*—for lack of a more mature way to put it—want for each other, *do* for each other. Just like *you* did for *me* when I was raging against the world over the death of my son."

"I think your grandson helped you through that," replied Sierra.

"Don't sell yourself short. The last couple of months have been hell on me. And simply having you with me, knowing you were there," he shook his head, "I may not have said it, but that meant a lot to me." Lockhart looked away, his mind going over the tough times he had just referenced. "In fact," a moment, "until now, I don't think I fully realized how much I needed you."

Sierra grew more mortified by the moment. She had totally misread the situation, misread his intentions. Perhaps part of the healing process, of overcoming a tragic experience, was to let others in, let others help you. Silently, she laughed at herself. She had said basically the same thing to him two months ago, after he had sent his fist through the glass on his gun cabinet. Sierra laid her hand on his forearm.

Feeling the pressure, Lockhart glimpsed the gesture then faced her.

She smiled at him. "I'm sorry," a pulse, "for jumping

to conclusions. Maybe I need to take a page out of your book and let you," she fumbled on the words her mind had queued up, *take care of me*, words that weren't comfortable for her, considering what she had endured at that cabin in New York, "maybe *we* need to take care of *each other*."

He laid his right hand on hers and gave it a gentle squeeze. "Deal."

CHAPTER 12
HEARTLESS

TWO HOURS LATER

An hour ago, back at his house, Lockhart had left Sierra the combination to the gun safe, along with a request for frequent updates on how she was doing. In response, she had told him, "I'll either call or text you every hour, *on* the hour. I promise." And to further ease his mind, she had followed up with, "Plus, I'm thinking of heading into Wyatt to do some shopping before my hair appointment. So, I'll be around plenty of people."

Lockhart had frowned. "Hair appointment? What's wrong with the way it is?"

"Sorry to disappoint, but," she had then toyed with her locks, saying, "I'm not a natural blonde. This is the work of a professional."

After scratching his chin and studying her hair some more, he had said, "That's okay. I like it blonde. Looks good." Following another moment, he had then added, "Shorter, though?"

"Oh, really," Sierra had shot back after picking up on his disapproving tone. "So, you like long hair, huh?"

Lockhart had then shrugged, "Longer the better, I always say," before adding a mischievous partial grin and leaving the house, leaving her with her arms folded, one hip thrown out to the side, and speechless.

Now, driving to Kellen Riley's residence, Lockhart sat behind the wheel of his Jeep Grand Wagoneer, holding his cell phone to his right cheek. "So, you're telling me this guy dressed up like one of our deputies to get Tricia Stefanik to open her hotel room door?"

Through his phone's speaker, Piper's voice: "I went over the hotel's security footage a dozen times last night. He came up through the back stairs and knocked on her door. It took me a few seconds to realize he *wasn't* one of our deputies. He had on a cowboy hat, tan shirt like we wear, blue jeans, and even a gun belt of sorts. The only thing out of place were his boots. They were construction-worker-type boots, but these ones looked new. They didn't have any of the usual scuff marks, dirt, grease—*whatever*—that you'd expect to find on boots worn by someone who does manual labor for a living." Piper took a breath. "Anyway, if Tricia had looked through her hotel room's peephole, she would have easily mistaken him for a real deputy."

Lockhart made a face and shook his head in disbelief. *This guy's a real pro. And heartless.*

"And he kept his head down the whole time to avoid the cameras," said the undersheriff. "His wide-brimmed hat helped with that, too."

"How long was he inside her room?"

"Time stamps show he entered at six-ten and left at

six-sixteen. That tracks with what the deputy on duty said as well. He last checked on Tricia a little before six." A beat. "Wade, our assassin was watching us. He knew exactly *when* and *how* to strike."

Lockhart scowled, his grip tightening on his phone and the steering wheel. He took it personally whenever people in his county got injured, lost their lives in accidents, fires, you name it. But murder victims propelled his self-reproach to a whole new level. Every moment he wasn't thinking about this case, he had been trying to figure out what he could have done differently, what tiny decision he could have made that would have saved Tricia Stefanik's life. Sure, she had been cheating on her husband, but that certainly didn't warrant her being executed. This was America, not first-century Jerusalem.

In the end, he consoled himself with the fact that despite his best efforts, he wasn't a superhero in some comic book. Real-life events didn't always have happy endings. And bad people, evil people, sometimes got away with doing bad things to others.

"Plus," continued Piper, "this guy had plenty of time to get to *your* place last night *after* he killed Tricia."

Lockhart grunted. "So, we still don't know who he is or what he looks like."

"That's correct."

"And Tricia never ID'd anyone from the photos she looked at yesterday?"

"The deputy who was with her said she picked out someone who *might* have looked *somewhat* like the man she saw at Pete McCord's place the night he was murdered. She said his baseball hat had been obscuring his face, though."

Might. Somewhat, he thought. "Not exactly solid testimony."

"I've gone ahead and put out a BOLO for the man she identified, anyway. I said to *approach with caution* in case he's not our man."

Lockhart stared at the road ahead, the rising sun just now cresting the black, jagged mountain peaks on his eleven o'clock. The pristine snow sparkled, as the sun's rays forced him to squint.

"Are you on your way into the Office?"

He lowered the Jeep's visor then rotated it toward his side window. "Making a stop at Kellen Riley's place first."

"What for?" she asked.

"See if I can wring water from a stone."

"Want me to back you up?"

"No," Lockhart replied. "This won't take long. He'll either cooperate or he won't."

"Yeah, it's that *he won't* part that's got me worried, especially after the way you embarrassed him last night."

"Just keep digging into Jace's reports. I'll be okay." He clicked off then made a right turn at the next cross street.

• • •

Fifteen Minutes Later...

With his Ruger Redhawk in his hands and angled downward, Lockhart used the toe of his boot to ease the ajar front door to Kellen Riley's house the rest of the way open.

Just inside the home, two men—the same two men who had confronted Lockhart at the strip club last night—lay face down in pools of blood that looked like dark-red halos around their heads.

Leading with his 44 Magnum, Lockhart cleared the family room and kitchen before taking the stairs to the second level. There, in a bedroom, he discovered two more shooting victims: a man, and a woman, both in various stages of undress. The male was on the bed while the female was sprawled halfway off the bed.

Retreating, the sheriff cleared a bathroom and a second bedroom before entering a third room and clearing what he could see. Holding his gun high, he approached a closed door, reached down with his left hand, then swung open the door while backtracking.

The interior was dark.

He clicked on his Pelican 2360 flashlight and curled into the space—into what turned out to be a cavernous walk-in closet—to point his Redhawk at nothing but two rows of clothing on hangers and multiple pairs of footwear lined up beneath the hanging apparel.

Lockhart spun left to stare at two dead bodies on a massive king-sized canopy bed. One was male, and the other was female. The dead woman, one he didn't know, was on top of a dead Kellen Riley. Belly to belly, both were naked and seemed to have been killed 'in the act.' The female victim had been shot in the right ear while the late Riley had a twenty-two-caliber bullet hole in his forehead.

Lockhart holstered his gun and hauled out his phone. "Piper, get a deputy out to Kellen Riley's place. I've got six dead bodies here."

Having left the murder scene in the hands of a deputy for processing, Lockhart had begun his journey back to the Sheriff's Office. Outside his Jeep, sunny skies had given way to clouds and light flurries, and the country road he was on already had a dusting on it.

Through his phone's speaker pressed to his left ear, Piper's voice: "While I was at Jace's desk, going through his reports, I broke a pencil. When I tried sharpening it, the sharpener on his desk just rumbled. So, figuring it needed cleaning, I picked it up and dumped out what must have been ten-years-worth of shavings inside the thing."

Lockhart inwardly groaned. When she had initially called, she had told him she had found something interesting. *Pencil shavings don't qualify as interesting, Piper.* He navigated the Jeep into a right-curving bend.

"When I went to put back the sharpener, I found something under where the sharpener had been setting on the desk, a tiny flash drive. It must've gotten shoved under there at some point, maybe when one of us was going through Jace's things. I don't know."

"What's on it?"

"A single file pertaining to that case from back in October. You know, the one involving those two young women? One ended up dying and the other was kidnapped and taken to that mountain cabin."

Lockhart knew the case well. He, Sierra, and Ranger had tracked the perpetrators—Dallas and Dawson Nash—to the cabin. Then, he and Sierra had been forced to shoot them when they had attempted to gun down the sheriff and the former police officer.

"Did you know Jace was conducting a side investigation into that case?" asked Piper.

Lockhart came out of the bend. "I had him pull some phone records, but I never authorized any side investigation."

"Well," she paused, "he was certainly doing more than pulling phone records."

Lockhart took a rise in the road. A second later, cresting the hill, he spotted two vehicles up ahead on the right side of the road. Both were parked bumper to bumper, and a man was standing over a jack by the car furthest away from Lockhart. "What was he doing?"

Piper huffed. "I'm not exactly sure, but I think you're going to want to see this for yourself."

Lockhart pulled up behind a black, four-door sedan. Ahead of it was a smaller-sized, blue, four-door SUV. "Have it ready for me when I get there." After closing his flip phone, he put the Grand Wagoneer in 'Park,' shut off the engine, and got out.

Strolling toward the vehicles, Lockhart recalled the stranded teenager who he had helped get his car started outside the bank in Adder. Even before he became sheriff, Lockhart would often stop to see if he could lend a hand. He wasn't a professional mechanic by any means. But he was good with his hands, and he knew enough about cars to be 'dangerous.' It was a combination that had served him well and had helped many other drivers along the way.

The man standing over the jack was dressed in a shorter-length leather jacket, blue jeans, and boots. He was now down on one knee, a tire iron in his hand, examining the jack.

"Hello there," called out Lockhart. "Sheriff's Office. Need some assistance?"

The man looked up and sighed a breath of relief. "Thank God." He stood and motioned behind him, toward a woman seated at the wheel of the disabled SUV. "She's got a flat, and I can't," he went from the tire iron to the jack, "seem to figure out this thing to save my soul."

Lockhart stopped near the man, glanced down at the flat tire, then spied the woman's reflection in the side-view mirror. "Yeah," he removed his Resistol, ran a hand over his hair, then settled the hat back onto his head, "sometimes these new contraptions can be confusing." He eyed the man, glimpsed the woman, then came back to him. "Are you two together?"

"No, I just stopped to see if I could help." The good Samaritan half smiled and lifted a shoulder before regarding the jack and the tool he held. "Guess I have my answer to that question."

Lockhart chuckled, "Hang tight," then strolled to the driver's door and knocked on the window.

In her forties, sporting a white winter jacket and short hair under a white woolen cap, she flinched when he rapped on the glass. She then rolled down her window and gave him a brief, crooked smile.

Lockhart glanced into the backseat then came back to her. "Are you okay, Ma'am?"

"Um," another awkward half grin, "yeah. Yeah, I...I just," she peeked at the side-view mirror, "I," then looked up at him, "I must've run over something in the road."

He peered at her, his gaze penetrating deeper to see what lay behind her blue eyes. After glimpsing the man who was still trying to unravel the jack mystery, the sheriff turned back to see that there were no keys in the ignition. Making eye contact with her, he tapped on her door. "Don't worry. I'll have you out of here in no time."

She dialed up another clumsy smile.

"Oh," he paused, "better roll up your window and lock your door, too." He glanced at the surrounding wilderness, tossing Good Samaritan a casual glance in the process. "Never know when a predator will jump out at you."

 RECKONING

She flicked her eyes toward GS, glimpsed Lockhart, then did as she was instructed.

Lockhart drew up on the man's left and glimpsed the jack. "Not really a handyman, huh?"

GS let out a short laugh. "Afraid not."

"What's your name?"

"Robert. Robert Williams."

Lockhart took off his jacket, made his way to the open rear hatch, and tossed the outerwear into the storage area. "What do you do for a living, Mr. Williams?"

"I'm an accountant."

"An accountant," repeated Lockhart. "Well, that explains why you're not good with your hands. *Numbers are your trade.*"

Williams nodded once. "They sure are."
"Also explains how you're able to," Lockhart gestured toward Williams' newer-looking work boots, "keep your boots there so clean."

Williams cocked his head then dialed up a nervous laugh. "Yeah, I," he glanced down while tapping the tire iron against his up-turned left palm, "I only wear these every once in a while." He came back to the sheriff.

Glimpsing white fur on the collar of Williams' jacket, Lockhart sized up the man. *He wasn't a big guy. But he wasn't skinny either. Not quite six feet tall.* Those were Tricia Stefanik's words, not Lockhart's. "How about you hand me that tire iron, Mr. Williams, and we can get this nice lady on her way?"

Williams eyeballed the black length of metal, angled at the end he had been tapping against his left palm, then squinted at his petitioner.

Lockhart noticed the man's eyes had changed. They were no longer the eyes of a man who had never gotten his hands dirty.

Williams reared back his right arm and swung the makeshift weapon toward the lawman.

Lockhart pulled down on the SUV's hatch and deflected the strike before backing up alongside the right-rear tire. "Get down on the floor," he shouted toward the woman while drawing his Ruger.

Williams drew a gun and fired while sidestepping toward the sedan.

Twenty-two-caliber bullets pinged off sheet metal.

Lockhart ducked. "Stay down, Ma'am!"

The sedan's engine started and revved before peeling away and roaring past the SUV.

Lockhart raised his Ruger and emptied the cylinder at the fleeing assassin.

The gun bellowed six times.

Six 44 Magnums slammed into the sedan, one projectile shattering the back window.

He got the woman's attention. "Are you okay?"

She nodded her head.

"Stay put. A sheriff's deputy will be here shortly." He bolted away from the SUV, hopped into his Jeep, and started the vehicle. Looking up ahead, his mind envisioning the landscape, the layout of the roads around here, he looked to his right, toward an open field of snow. After another glance at the fugitive's sedan, he ran the gearshift to 'Drive' and drove into the field on his two o'clock.

• • •

One Minute Later...

Having bounced over and plowed through several inches of snow, while shooting glances toward his ten o'clock all the while, Lockhart now goosed the Jeep's accelerator.

Building speed, the Grand Wagoneer ascended a sharp rise. Halfway up, the vehicle slowed and fishtailed but kept on climbing.

At the top of the hill, Lockhart cranked the wheel to the left and stopped the SUV twenty feet later. He pressed a button, hopped out, and trudged through snow to get to the tailgate. The tailgate's window was already on the way down.

He reached into the cargo area, retrieved his Henry Big Boy Steel Side Gate lever action rifle, also chambered in 44 Magnum, then climbed on top of the Jeep's roof.

Off in the distance, on his eleven o'clock, the sedan had come out of a curve and was now gaining speed on a straightaway that went from Lockhart's left to right.

Dropping to his knees, Lockhart then went prone

and put the Henry to his left shoulder. After spreading his feet and glancing at how the snow was floating down, he cocked the gun's hammer and acquired the sedan in the Big Boy's sights.

A hundred yards ahead of the sedan, a thick stand of trees would swallow up his target in seconds.

He took a breath, held it, then let out half. Adjusting for the wind, and vehicle speed, he took aim and touched his left index finger to the trigger.

Fifty yards.

Lockhart closed his right eye and focused on centering the Big Boy's bead front sight inside the gun's rear peep sight.

Thirty yards.

He pulled the gun deeper into his shoulder, made one last alteration to his sight alignment, then applied consistent pressure to the trigger.

Twenty yards.

The Henry boomed, spewing out a 240-grain hollow soft point bullet.

Ten yards from the tree line, the sedan swerved right and left before doing a clockwise three-sixty and sliding off the road.

Back at the scene of the firefight; specifically, the long shot from the roof of his Jeep, Lockhart's aim had been true. A 44 Magnum bullet had blown a hole in the speeding sedan's right-front tire. The snowy road conditions had done the rest. The vehicle had gone airborne, rolling twice in the air, before slamming into a tree trunk and coming to rest upside down. An ambulance had then rushed the unconscious assassin, who had sustained a serious head injury in the crash, to the nearest hospital.

Lockhart had then learned from the woman in the SUV that the man had run her off the road, put a gun to her head, and then snatched her keys from the ignition. After having taken her cell phone and telling her to play along if she wanted to live, he had then stuck a knife into the SUV's left-rear tire, opened the rear hatch, then laid out the jack and tire iron. The woman said two cars had stopped, their owners offering assistance, but the assassin had waved them off, telling them he had everything under control.

Now, standing beside Piper's desk, a seated Piper on

his left, Lockhart spread out several photos on her desk. "These were in the possession of our assassin." He had already told her what took place along the side of the road. He pointed. "Here's Pete McCord and," his finger went to a second photo, "here's Kellen Riley," before he tapped a third photograph. "I'm thinking this is the man who hired Riley. Whoever he is, he might be the guy who initially took out the contract on Jace."

"Unless he's another cutout," countered Piper, as she wiggled a pencil in her grasp.

"That'll be our first question after you find out who he is and put a BOLO out on him." He laid his hands on his hips. "Now what about this side investigation of Jace's you mentioned?"

Piper brought up the file on the tiny flash drive she had found on Jace's desk. "He had one of those boards you—" She pushed papers aside on her desk, snatched three pieces of paper, and, "Here," handed them to her boss. "I know how you prefer things to be on paper rather than computers."

He claimed the sheets and perused them while she spoke.

She went back to eyeing her computer screen. "As you can see, Jace had one of those boards you see on cop shows."

Lockhart noticed different words, names, places on the first page with lines connecting those words, names, and places. "Uh-huh."

"He also had his own," she held up a hand, palm up, "notes, speculations, whatever you want to call them," a beat, "on how he thought all these things were connected." Piper got up, hoisted her gun belt higher up her waist, then stood shoulder to shoulder with Lockhart, he on her right, as she used her pencil to point out things on the page he held. "Now, most of this doesn't make sense to me. Jace is the only one who knew how these pieces fit together. *But*," she tapped a number on the paper, "this is a cell number that belongs to one of the four phones we recovered from that mountain cabin. Remem—"

"The cabin we tracked Dallas and Dawson Nash to."

"Exactly," affirmed the undersheriff. "So, remember how we thought four people up there, four phones, one for each person?"

"Uh-huh."

"Not so."

He frowned. "What do you mean?"

"One belonged to Dallas, one belonged to one of the men who met the Nash brothers there, and *two* belonged to Dawson. One was registered in his name with a cell carrier. But I tracked the second to a store in Idaho, where the owner accepted a credit card payment from—"

"Dawson Nash," interjected Lockhart.

Piper pointed the pencil at him. "Correct."

"Why would he have two phones on him?"

"Great question. I asked myself that same thing." She

intertwined her forearms, threw out her right hip, and faced him. "Do you remember when Ginnie Henderson said she heard one of the Nash brothers make a call...when she was tied up in the back of that Jimmy?"

Lockhart nodded. "Dawson probably used the burner he had to make that call, so it couldn't be traced back to him."

"That's what I thought, too." Piper pivoted toward her desk, scooped up more pieces of paper, and spun back toward him. "But these phone records Jace got show a call was placed from Dawson's," she wavered, "let's call it his *main* phone *to*," she tapped the page Lockhart held, pointing at a different cell number, "that number there."

"Who does *that* number belong to?"

She held a shrug. "I don't know. I'm assuming it's another burner. But where I'm heading with this is that the call falls within the timeline of when Ginnie said she was in the back of that Jimmy. So, I'm thinking, when Dawson made that call that night—to whoever—in the heat of the moment, he probably messed up and used his *main* phone. Because when I checked his burner, the call log *hadn't* been wiped, and there was *no* record of any calls, outgoing or incoming, during that time."

Wincing, Lockhart rubbed his eyes. "Tie down this calf for me, Piper. We know Dawson called *someone*. But what does that have to do with *this* case, with finding whoever took out the hit on Jace?"

"I haven't figured that out yet, but," she pointed out a

name beside the number that Dawson had called, "I think *Jace* had a suspect in mind."

Lockhart squinted at the name at the end of her finger. Three question marks had been scribbled to the right of that name. Lockhart stared straight ahead then observed his undersheriff.

She raised her eyebrows while cocking her head to the side. "It's worth looking into, don't you think?"

Lockhart got out of his Jeep, slammed the door, and marched up the driveway before cutting left and taking a winding, brick pathway to the right, toward a century-old two-story home.

The home was constructed of fat, horizontally placed logs with stone columns supporting an A-framed, covered front porch. The front door was four-feet-wide and eight-feet-tall, made of solid oak, and had an inlaid glass decoration near the top. A padded wooden bench ran the full width of the eight-foot-wide window to the right of the massive door and stopped where an old wooden rocker sat.

Lockhart took the single step to the front porch. A wood handrail on his three o'clock spanned the distance from him to the attached garage further away on his right. On his immediate left, the home's horizontal logs jutted six feet away from the front wall before making a ninety-degree turn toward Lockhart's nine o'clock. Overhead, a copper wagon-wheel chandelier hung horizontally from chains and had thin copper figures of elk, bear, and pine trees rising toward the ceiling.

The sheriff of Big Sky County ignored the door

buzzer mounted on the jamb and pounded on the door with his fist. When he got no reply, he banged on the door again, harder this time. "Sheriff's Office. Open the door!"

Two seconds later, the door opened, and a man wearing blue jeans, brown cowboy boots, and a black button-up dress shirt—the top two buttons undone to show off gray chest hairs—stepped outside. At 45 years old, the six-foot, 185-pound man had a baldhead and mustache, and displayed a trim, muscled build with a slight paunch.

The two men knew each other from their youthful days to the election for sheriff six years ago, when Lockhart had bested the man and assumed the role of Big Sky County Sheriff.

"What do *you* want?" said Baxter Nash while slipping thumbs into his waistband, his fingers bookending a silver-colored belt buckle. In the center of that rounded rectangular buckle was the ornate scrolling of the letter 'N' done in gold.

"We need to talk," said Lockhart.

"About *what*?"

"I'd prefer to do this inside."

Baxter reached back, grabbed the doorknob, and pulled.

The heavy door closed with a bang.

"You're no longer welcome in my house. Whatever you have to say," Baxter pointed at the concrete ahead of the thick, black mat he was standing on, "you'll say it out here."

"Very well then." Lockhart placed his hands on his hips and shifted his weight to his left foot. "I'm just going to come out with it. Did you have my son killed?"

Baxter's head recoiled an inch while his brows shot upward. He huffed in the next instant, looking away and rubbing a hand down his face.

Lockhart studied him, studied his motions, dissecting every little facial tick he spotted, watching for, and maybe even hoping for, a telltale sign the man was prepping a lie. But all the man's physical motions were disguising whatever signs he may have been giving off.

Baxter shook his head. "If memory serves, Wade, you *caught* the man who killed your son."

"I didn't ask you if *you* killed him. I asked if you *had* him killed."

"What the *hell* are you talking about?"

Lockhart noted the man's anger. Whether it was genuine or fake, anger was a good way to cover up a lie. "Jace uncovered something about your boys. He found out that Dawson had two phones on him the night that he and Dallas kidnapped Ginnie Henderson. One was his normal phone, and the other was an untraceable burner phone. Trouble is, though, when he called you for help, he used the wrong one. He used his normal one."

Baxter crossed his arms over his chest and stared at his opponent down the length of his nose. "I told you I never received any calls from either of my sons that night."

"That's what you *said*. But Jace got a hold of Dawson's phone records and discovered a call was made right around the time Ginnie Henderson was tied up in the back of your son's vehicle."

Baxter nodded. "If that's true, then prove it. Prove he called me that night." He held his arms out to his sides, palms up. "Show me the evidence. Hell, you can even check *my* phone records if that'll help. I won't stop you."

Lockhart scratched his chin while eyeballing his nemesis. He and Piper had already called the number, only to get the announcement that the number was 'no longer in service.'

He jabbed a finger at Baxter's chest. "That's what you and Jace were discussing at The Buckin Bronco, wasn't it?"

The county commissioner frowned. "What?"

"The surveillance video of you two talking, two days before Jace was gunned down. That's what you two were talking about."

Baxter set his jaw.

"He confronted you about him having knowledge of your involvement in your sons' crimes."

Baxter crossed his arms again and stared at the toes of his boots.

"Knowing my son, I'll bet he told you something along the lines that he would never stop digging into what actually happened that night. Even if it killed him, he would uncover the truth." Lockhart heard his words again. *And it did get him killed.*

Still looking down, Baxter shook his head.

"And you knew the truth was going to lead right...straight...back...to *you.*"

Baxter chuckled at first. Then his laughter grew before subsiding. "Oh, Wade, you've really lost it, you know that? Your kid's murder has really," he made gestures near his head, "messed with your mind, hasn't it?" He huffed. "And I thought I had it tough when you murdered my boys."

"I never murdered them, Bax. I was—"

"You were *what?*" shouted Baxter. "Saving the girl? Saving Big Sky from two vicious men terrorizing the good citizens of the county? No." He thrust out his index finger, stopping an inch from the sheriff's chest. "*You,*" spittle shot out of his mouth as he went on, "*murdered* them in *cold blood.* That's what you did." He waved a hand. "There's no other way you can spin that, Sheriff Lockhart."

Lockhart plopped hands onto his hips again and looked away.

"Ever since high school," continued Baxter, "ever since you stole Cheryl from me, you've had it in for me."

Lockhart whipped his head toward the raging man.

"I thought I was done with you when you joined the military. But then you had to come back here and run for sheriff and steal one more thing away from me. Then," Baxter laughed out loud, "then, you had to take those last two things in my life that were the most precious to me. You gunned them down in cold blood." He sent his index finger toward Lockhart's eyes. "Because you're a *murderer*, Wade."

Lockhart brushed aside the accusations. They were the rantings of a mad man. But his mind did settle on one thing this mad man had mentioned. "I never *stole* Cheryl away from you." He pointed at his sternum. "She *chose* me. Her and I getting together had *nothing* to do with you. That's what happens in life. People meet and either fall in love or move on to someone else. She moved on from you and ended up marrying *me*."

Grinding his teeth and shaking his head, Baxter made fists. "And if she hadn't ended up marrying you, she would still be *alive* today."

Lockhart lunged forward and grabbed Baxter by the shirt collar. "Don't you ever—"

Baxter broke Lockhart's hold and pushed the lawman backward.

Lockhart slammed into the eighteen-inch-square stone column attached to the handrail.

"Don't what?" bellowed Baxter. "Speak the truth?" He wagged his finger at his counterpart. "Don't you ever come onto *my* property and lay hands on me again. I don't care if you *are* the sheriff. I'll kill you where you stand."

Lockhart stood tall. "Words from someone capable of murdering another man's son."

"You would know," shot back Baxter before he bit down and bared his teeth at his accuser. "Tell me something, Wade. When you go to bed at night, when your head hits that pillow, and you close your eyes," Baxter glared at Lockhart, "which do you see first," a beat, "your dead wife's mangled body or your son's *face* blown to bits?"

Making fists, Lockhart took a step toward Baxter before catching himself, checking his instinct to retaliate.

This interrogation of a potential suspect had devolved into a shouting match between two men, two rivals from childhood. And the shouting match was a few choice words away from becoming a physical, violent altercation, something the sheriff of Big Sky County could not afford to let happen.

With no more investigative avenues to pursue, issues to press the commissioner on, Lockhart adjusted the Resistol on his head, gave Baxter a last stare, then stepped off the porch.

One mile down the road from Baxter Nash's home, Lockhart gripped the Grand Wagoneer's steering wheel a little tighter as he spoke into his cell phone. "Turn over every stone, Piper. I don't care how long it takes or how much it costs. Baxter's involved in all this. I know it."

"Since he's a county commissioner, we're going to need some heavy evidence, Wade."

"Then we'll *get* it. Check his phone records. Check his business dealings. Dig into his financial statements. Heck, go down to the courts and—" Lockhart slammed on the brakes.

The Jeep fishtailed to the left before stopping in the roadway, its driver staring through its windshield.

Lockhart's right arm slowly fell to his right thigh, as his mind revisited yesterday afternoon's phone call with Judge Thomas. *I appreciate you considering this matter. I'll wait for your decision before submitting my official report.*

Piper's faint voice came from the cell phone he held. "Wade? Did I lose you? Are you still there?"

"Son-of-a—" he tossed the phone onto the passenger seat and cranked the steering wheel all the way to the left.

The Jeep went into the oncoming lane, onto the snow-covered shoulder, then back onto the roadway.

Lockhart straightened out the wheel, stomped on the gas pedal, and steered the vehicle back the way he had come.

• • •

One Minute Later...

Lockhart entered the driveway on 'two wheels' before hitting the brakes and running the gearshift to 'Park,' leaving the Jeep sitting cockeyed in the driveway.

He got out, slammed his door shut, and strode toward the front door.

Gunshots rang out from the home as bullets penetrated the front window and zipped by Lockhart's head.

He ducked then dove for cover behind an earthen mound on the home's front lawn. The snowy, decorative landscape wasn't much, but it at least put something between him and the incoming rounds.

Bullets kept coming his way, sending puffs of snow upward near his boots.

On his back, he drew his Ruger Redhawk.

More reports came from inside the house.

Five-five-six, he thought, his mind placing the caliber of the gun being used against him. *AR-15.* He surveyed his surroundings and saw his only escape, except for a head-on charge, which was suicide, was to work his way around to the side of the house, on his Jeep's ten o'clock, and move along the structure's front, back toward his Jeep.

Three more bullets broke more glass on their way toward Lockhart.

He barrel-rolled to his right several times, staying below the mound's crest.

Three rolls in, his hat fell off.

When he had put a lone pine tree between him and the window, he went to a crouch, then rose up and sprinted for the corner of the house, his left shoulder ramming into the horizontal logs a few seconds later.

Staying below two smaller, separate windows, which were higher up on the house, he worked his way to where the logs jutted out from the front wall, left of the front door. After sizing up the massive door, anticipating that it would be locked, he emptied his Ruger at the space above the doorknob.

Splinters flew everywhere, as six 44 Magnums tore hunks of wood from the door.

Lockhart opened his Ruger's cylinder and smacked the gun's ejector rod with his right palm.

Six empty cases fell into the snow.

He retrieved a speedloader from his coat pocket, lined up the six bullets with the six empty chambers, and pushed the reloading device until all six cartridges released, dropping into place. He stowed the empty speedloader, peeked at the door again, then peeled away from cover.

Charging onto the porch, he raised his right foot and sent a boot into the door.

The heavy door flew inward and bounced off an interior wall.

With his Redhawk up and pointed ahead of him, Lockhart barged into Baxter Nash's home.

•••

Five Minutes Later...

Sierra pulled up behind Lockhart's SUV in her red, four-door Jeep Wrangler Sport, Ranger in the cargo area. She looked. She listened. She waited. Nothing. No movement, no sounds anywhere.

Shouldering her door open, she climbed out and drew her Smith & Wesson Shield Plus from a holster under her coat, on the right side of her belt. Creeping forward, she pulled up at the Grand Wagoneer. After peeking through the driver's window, she opened the door, leaned in, and snatched a flip phone from off the passenger seat. "Piper?" she said, putting the mobile to her left ear.

Piper's voice: "Sierra? Did you find him?"

"His car's here, and his phone's here, but *he's* not."

"Damn it. Any signs of a gunfight?"

Sierra squinted at the house, her eyes settling on the broken front window and the open front door. "Yeah." Her heart was in her throat now. "I'm thinking so." She swallowed the 'lump' and focused on Piper. "What did you hear?"

"He was talking to me and then just stopped. I thought we lost the connection. The next thing I heard were gunshots, high-pitched ones, coming through the phone. A minute later, I heard six big booms and then nothing. That's why I called you from my desk phone. I wanted to keep this line open." Piper cursed three times in a row. "See what you can find. I'm still," a pause, "over thirty minutes away."

"Okay," replied Sierra. "Drive safe." She disconnected the call, thinking to herself how stupid it was to tell a cop to drive safely when her partner might be in trouble. She herself would have broken every speed record there was to get to her partner, even more if Wade were in trouble.

Out of the corner of her eye, Sierra saw something black on the front lawn. She started toward the object then stopped, changing course a moment later and heading toward the rear of her vehicle.

. . .

Two Minutes Later...

A leash in her left hand, the leash attached to Ranger's harness, Sierra picked up Lockhart's black Resistol hat from off the front lawn. "Ranger, on me."

The dog sat facing his handler.

"Time to work."

He stood.

She held out Lockhart's hat.

The GSD sniffed it, sticking his snout deep inside.

She let out some of his leash and said, "Seek, Ranger. Seek!"

Ranger lowered his nose to the snow and darted back and forth, sniffing where the hat had been found. He lifted his head and pointed it in different directions before lowering it again and trotting toward the house. He made a right and jogged along the front of the structure, making a left at another corner before going through the front door.

Sierra trailed her dog, the leash in her left hand, and her Shield in the other. Stepping into the darkened home, with Ranger tugging on the leash, she aimed her gun in all directions, as the K-9 team cleared the living room.

A minute later, after having passed straight through the house, through a set of double doors, and onto a back deck, Ranger and Sierra were now following tire tracks in the snow, tracks seemingly made by two separate vehicles. The trails followed the downward-sloping terrain that led to a valley before rising again toward a picturesque mountain miles away. Leafless trees and dark-green evergreens, their boughs full of snow and hanging low, also followed the grade.

A hundred yards down the path, Sierra and Ranger stopped when three high-pitched guns shots were followed by two larger booms a few seconds later. She let out her GSD's leash and thrust out her right arm in the direction of the gunshots. "Ranger, go!"

The 90-pound dog ran ahead of her.

Sierra did her best to keep up with him, to stay on the trail, a trail that appeared to have been made by all-terrain vehicles of some sort. But Ranger tugged on the leash and veered left and right, forcing to trudge through snow at times, powdery snow that came halfway up her black-and-brown, knee-high hiking boots.

Up ahead, another exchange of gunfire sounded.

With her heart pounding and her breathing heavy from having to raise her boots so high with every stride, Sierra heard a voice in her head, a weary voice telling her to stop and rest. She ignored it, and the pain in her side, too, and slogged onward.

• • •

After having barged into Baxter's home and carefully cleared the main floor, Lockhart had then heard the growl of an engine outside. Running onto the back deck, he had seen Baxter on a red three-wheeler, an AR-15 rifle strapped across his back, racing away from a pole building in the backyard.

Finding a second all-terrain vehicle in the pole building, Lockhart had chased after the man.

A quarter mile later, after having zoomed in and out

of tree stands, Lockhart had entered a clearing to find the three-wheeler had overturned and was laying upside down further down the slope to his right.

Gunshots had then sounded from up the hill to his left, from somewhere among the trees, forcing him to seek cover behind his four-wheeler.

Now, for the last few minutes, the men had exchanged gunfire. With Lockhart's rate of fire limited by his revolver, he could only get off one round to Baxter's three or four rounds.

Lying on his left side, behind the four-wheeler's right-rear tire, Lockhart was in a similar predicament to what he had faced on the front lawn, namely pinned down by a rifleman with nowhere to go.

Three rounds of incoming five-five-six pinged off metal. Earlier rounds had flattened both tires on the vehicle's left side. So, riding his way out of this was not an option for the sheriff.

Lockhart topped off his Ruger with three cartridges he plucked from the loops securing the ammo to the brown leather ammo slide riding on his belt at the five o'clock position. He closed the gun's cylinder, looked up at a sky of patchy clouds, then exhaled, sending a cloud of water vapor into the air. "Give it up, Bax," he shouted. "You're not getting out of this. I know you had my son killed."

No reply.

"Other than my undersheriff and less than a handful

of trusted people, no one knew the details of Jace's death, not even the news media. And I've been petitioning the courts to keep it that way. Hell, I haven't even submitted my official report yet." Lockhart filled his lungs and exhaled. "So, the only way you could've known that—as *you* put it—that Jace's face was blown to bits, was if you were in contact with the killers."

Five seconds passed.

Baxter's voice: "I knew the moment I said that I had messed up. Heat of the moment, I guess. You didn't seem to catch it, so I thought maybe the gods were smiling down on me."

"No. I doubt God is smiling on you," replied Lockhart. "So, tell me. Why'd you do it? Revenge?"

Three seconds.

"Revenge was simply the sweet aftertaste. No, your kid was connecting the dots between me and my boys taking that stupid girl. He came to me with," a beat, "with some damn phone records he'd gotten hold of." Baxter laughed. "Technology. Hurts us more than it helps us. Anyway, I knew it was only a matter of time before he uncovered the truth. Hell, I'm surprised he never told *you* what he had discovered."

Lockhart swallowed down a wave of remorse. *I wish he HAD. Maybe I could've—* Lockhart closed his eyes and drove away the thought. Opening his eyes a moment later, he raised his voice. "Lose the gun and come down with your hands up. I give you my word I won't shoot you." A beat. "That's more than you gave my son."

"I don't want your word, Wade. Your word means nothing to me. I'm just happy I was able to take something from *you* the way you took my boys from *me*."

Lockhart squeezed the Redhawk's Hogue Monogrip a little harder.

"No. I want you to live the rest of your life, wondering if there was anything you could have done to save your kid. That's what I want from you. I want you to suffer, knowing you'll never ever see him again, knowing you'll never ever hear his voice again..."

Clenching his teeth...

"...knowing you'll never ever—"

...Lockhart peeked above the four-wheeler's seat and let loose with three rounds of 44 Magnum before ducking back down.

Baxter laughed. "What's the matter, Wade? Is the guilt setting in already?" More laughter was followed by a string of five-five-six gunfire.

Lockhart ducked down further as bullets tore up his cover a little more.

• • •

Wearing Lockhart's black cowboy hat, Sierra was still trying to catch her breath from her run through deep snow. Now, with her knees bent, she slow walked up a slight hillside, her Shield 9mm in both hands and pointing straight ahead of her.

Ranger was off leash and walking between her legs, keeping pace with his handler's gait, both human and animal moving as one.

With her left hand, she reached down and palmed his nose.

He looked back at her.

She lowered her flat left hand to the snow, and Ranger laid down between her legs as she went to her right knee, her left boot beside his left shoulder. In this position, with him out of her line of sight, she had plenty of room to shoot over his head if necessary.

She took in a few more gulps of air, trying to slow her breathing, as her pulse returned to normal.

Baxter's voice: "Is the guilt setting in already?"

More than a hundred yards away, rifle fire sounded.

Ranger tensed.

With her left hand, Sierra crossed over his body and patted his right shoulder. The simple act let him know she was calm and that he should be, too.

The recently commissioned Big Sky County K-9 team was on the edge of a tree line. If they went any further, they would risk exposing themselves to the enemy.

The ex-cop calculated a shot from this distance. Bullet drop would easily be a foot, maybe more. She'd have to hold her Smith & Wesson's sights above her target. Even for a professional, a shot like this would be tough. *Then again*, she thought, looking toward her one o'clock, down the slope, to see Lockhart hiding behind the ATV, *maybe I don't need to actually HIT my target.* She came back to her eleven o'clock, further up the grade, and spied the grouping of trees Baxter was using for cover. *Just rattle his cage.*

• • •

One to two seconds apart, the consistent sound of faraway 'pops' drew Lockhart's attention. On his back, he rolled his head to the right. Another 'pop' helped him zero in on the source.

Just inside the tree line, more than a hundred yards away, with a dark-colored dog lying between her legs and a black cowboy hat on her head, a crouching blonde-haired woman was firing a pistol toward Baxter's hiding place.

Lockhart squinted at the woman. *Sierra.* He didn't know how she had found him, but he took what she was doing for what it was, a diversion, covering fire. He sprang to his feet and ran up the hill. Darting right, then left, zigging and zagging so the man couldn't get a clean shot on him, he fired his Ruger toward Baxter's place among the trees.

Halfway up the incline, the Redhawk ran dry.

Continuing to snake his way toward his adversary, he opened the cylinder and used his left thumb to eject the cases while pulling a speedloader from a pouch at the four o'clock position on his belt.

With the revolver up and running, Lockhart raced onward, firing three more rounds as he drew within ten feet of the trees.

The nine-millimeter reports coming from his left ceased.

His diversion, his covering fire, was over. There was no way Sierra would risk a shot now that he was so close to her target.

Lockhart ducked into the forest and found the nearest tree to hide behind. He peeked out but saw nothing. Moving right and curling to his left, he came to a stretch of flat land. A few steps later, after peering over the side of a cliff on his right, and seeing a shallow drop-off, he faced forward, squeezed between some waist-high brush, then quickly raised his gun.

Fifteen feet ahead, Baxter was lying on his right side, a black rifle just outside his reach. Propped up on his right elbow, he was bleeding from his left leg while his left hand covered another gunshot wound to his right side. Fortunately for him, this one was from a nine-millimeter pistol, and had only grazed him. The wound hurt, but he would live. The leg wound, however, was from a 44 Magnum that had broken his tibia. There was zero chance he was walking out of here under his own power.

Lockhart inched forward, kicked the AR-15 to the side, then stood six feet away from the man who had ordered the assassination of his son.

Both men simply stared at each other, each one seemingly recalling the events that had led to this moment in time, including their younger days, days spent competing on the football field in high school and taking one-two finishes in rodeo events.

A minute later, with Ranger walking between her legs, Sierra drew up on Lockhart's four o'clock, her Shield aimed at Baxter. "Ranger, down."

The dog laid down.

She lowered her firearm then gave each man a couple back-and-forth glances, finally settling on Lockhart. "Wade? What's going on?"

He said nothing. He just kept glaring at the downed man, his Ruger in his right hand, and pointed right at Baxter's face.

"What's going on, dearie," said Baxter, "is that your boyfriend here is trying to decide if he wants to arrest me or kill me."

Sierra eyed Lockhart. "Wade?"

Baxter shifted his position on the ground, going into a more upright stance while still resting on his right elbow.

His ears up, Ranger cocked his head at the man, barked twice, then bit the back of the sheriff's right calf.

Lockhart's right leg buckled. He caught himself then glanced down at the dog. "I see you, okay? Relax." Sierra had told him that the dog did stuff like that whenever he wanted someone to know he was there.

"Ranger, down," commanded Sierra.

The GSD laid down on Lockhart's three o'clock, his focus going from Baxter to Lockhart. In the next instant, he nipped at the sheriff's leg again.

Having seen her dog take the second bite, Sierra came up on Ranger's right, her pistol now down by her right thigh. "Ranger, stop." She then gave Lockhart a side-eye peek. "Maybe he's just trying to keep you from doing something stupid."

Standing, Ranger barked at Baxter again, sunk his teeth into Sierra's left boot, then retreated while tugging on her leg.

"Ranger," she said, throwing out an arm and taking an awkward step to keep from falling over, "down."

Reluctantly, the dog obeyed his handler.

"What have you decided, Wade?" asked Baxter.

Lockhart said nothing.

Seconds later, Baxter shook his head. "Maybe this will help." He turned over his right hand.

Lockhart stiffened when he saw an M67 grenade in Baxter's palm. Both the safety clip and the safety pin were missing. The only thing holding the 'spoon' in place, and keeping the device from detonating, was the man's fingers.

"Oh, my—" uttered Sierra, her heart rate spiking, as she raised her Shield toward the man again.

Lockhart reached over and pushed her arm back

down.

"That's right," said a sneering Baxter. "Shoot me, and we all go boom." He eyed Lockhart. "Arrest me, and I'm sure I won't be able to hold on to this."

Lockhart breathed deeply, his mind searching for another alternative. "I thought you said you wanted me to live, to suffer. Killing me won't accomplish that."

Baxter shrugged his left shoulder. "We can't get everything we want in life." He jerked his head toward Sierra. "Knowing I will have taken out your girlfriend, along with *you*, will have to suffice."

"Don't do this, Bax." Lockhart saw himself shooting the man in the head, grabbing the grenade, and tossing it. He had four to five seconds once the safety lever came off the grenade. After he shot Baxter, he would lose a second or two just getting to the grenade. Inwardly, he grimaced. *Two seconds to toss it and get clear.*

"I don't want to, Wade," replied Baxter, "but you leave me with no choice. If you had just left things well enough alone, you'd at least still have," he glimpsed Sierra then returned to Lockhart, "your new girlfriend."

Lockhart saw that the man's grip on the M67 had changed, *He's going to let go of it*, and he knew he had no other choice. He had to shoot him then throw the grenade as far away as he could.

"But as it stands now," continued Baxter.

Having been silently scooting over the snow on his belly, inching his way closer to the prone man, Ranger now sprang forward and threw himself at Baxter.

"You'll—"

The GSD clamped down on the man's right wrist, his teeth sinking into flesh.

Baxter bellowed.

Lockhart shoved Sierra. "Get down!"

Falling over the cliff on her right, she landed in soft snow, tumbled down the slope, and came to rest fifteen feet below the out-of-sight men, and her dog, above.

Ranger growled while whipping his head back and forth, tearing muscles in his prey's arm.

On his back now, Baxter swung his right arm forward and hit the animal with his closed hand and the fourteen-ounce grenade he held.

The safety lever came loose.

Ranger held on.

Watching the 'spoon' fall into the snow, Lockhart lunged forward. From behind, he wrapped his arms around Ranger's underbelly. Operating on pure adrenaline, he scooped the 90-pound brute off the ground and bolted toward the same cliff Sierra had gone over. Something heavy hit him between the shoulder blades as he took his last step before leaping into the air.

Man, and beast, touched down a second later, both rolling as one before Ranger caught his balance first. Lockhart continued for another five feet. Coming out of a roll, he spotted Sierra, pushed off, and dove on top of her.

Up above, a deafening blast sounded, sending a wash of snow and dirt outward and upward.

Particles and grit rained down on the trio.

Lockhart lifted his head to see a haze of white smoke being carried away on the wind. He faced Sierra. "Are you okay?"

Blinking her eyes while opening and closing her jaw a few times, she swallowed, then nodded her head. "I-I think so. Yeah. You?"

"I'm good." He crawled off her and climbed the hill, stretching out his left hand when he got to Ranger. "How about you? You good, too?"

The dog shook his head and body free of snow then licked Lockhart's palm.

"Ranger," cried Sierra.

"He's okay," shouted Lockhart before he swung his left arm down the grade. "Go. Stay with her."

The dog bounded down the hill toward Sierra.

Lockhart finished his ascent and peeked over the edge of the cliff. With his Ruger in both hands, he aimed it at a writhing Baxter Nash.

Somehow, the man had survived his own grenade attack. But he now had a few more injuries to go with his bullet wounds. The left side of the man's face was raw, the skin there having peeled away.

Lockhart had seen combat, seen dismembered and battle-scarred soldiers. That was another time, though. He was far enough removed from the battlefront that seeing Baxter in this condition made his stomach churn. Confident the commissioner was no longer a menace, Lockhart holstered his weapon, turned, and headed back toward Sierra and Ranger.

•••

One Hour Later...

Forty-five minutes ago, Piper had arrived at the scene and followed the ATV tracks in her Dodge Ram 1500 SSV (Special Service Vehicle). After caring for their prisoner's wounds as best they could, she and Lockhart had then loaded a handcuffed Baxter Nash into the bed of the truck.

Returning to Nash's driveway, where an ambulance had been waiting, Piper, Lockhart, Sierra, and Ranger had stood by while medical personnel tended to Baxter's injuries. Afterward, they loaded him into the ambulance and drove away, Piper riding in back with one of the EMTs.

Now, standing between the rear bumper of his Jeep Grand Wagoneer and the front bumper of Sierra's Jeep Wrangler Sport—after having reclaimed his Resistol, following a compliment on how the hat had looked on her—Lockhart glimpsed Ranger then squinted at Sierra. "Where'd you two come from, anyway? How'd you know where I was?"

She gestured toward the departing ambulance. "Piper

called me on my way back from the salon. She said she was talking to you on the phone, and that you just *stopped* talking. Then she heard gunfire. She was more than a half an hour away, and the only other available deputy was dealing with a horrific car accident. So, when I found out where you were, I told her I was nearby and that I would head right there. After all, as a full-fledged deputy now, aren't I supposed to have your back?"

He slipped his left arm around her waist and pulled her close. "And I yours, Deputy Courtright." His attention then went higher up, and he noticed her blonde hair was a brighter shade of blonde. "Your hair looks nice," a tick, "and shiny, too."

She spun her head left and right one time. "Thank you."

He made a face. "Doesn't look like she cut it at all."

"That's because she *didn't*," replied Sierra, twisting her body to nudge him with her shoulder, "you big baby, you."

He frowned. "Me? What did I do?"

"Because of what you said to me this morning, I told her to just trim up the ends, that I was planning to let it grow longer."

Recalling his parting words to her, *Longer the better, I always say*, he held back a snicker but couldn't keep a grin from materializing.

"So, yes, I didn't get it cut for *you*," said Sierra, playfully scolding him, "you big baby."

"Well, it looks great." A moment later, Lockhart's attention shifted to Ranger, who was sitting and looking up at him. "So, let me get this straight." Recalling how the animal had twice nipped the back of his calf, and Sierra's words that had followed, *Maybe he's just trying to keep you from doing something stupid*, Lockhart motioned behind him, toward where he had arrested Baxter. "You can *bite* the bad guys, but I can't *shoot* them?"

Sierra regarded her dog, a grin on her face.

With his mouth open, mimicking a smile, Ranger stared at his questioner. Two seconds later, his right eye closed then immediately opened.

Lockhart cocked his head, glanced at Sierra, then faced the dog. "Did he just…"

"You know," her smile blossomed as she admired her GSD, "he's done that to me on many occasions. And his timing is usually spot-on with whatever the situation happens to be." She shook her head. "Makes me think he understands more than we humans give him credit for."

Lockhart took a knee.

Ranger approached, his ears back, his tail wagging.

Lockhart ruffled the dog's fur then took the animal's head in both hands to peer into his amber-colored eyes. "No. You weren't worried about me shooting someone." He patted the dog between the ears. "You knew that guy was bad news, and you just wanted us out of there, didn't you?"

Sierra joined her man in stroking Ranger's long coat.

She observed the interaction between the two 'men' who had become close to one another in the last few months. And seeing that relationship bloom had warmed her heart. She leaned in and kissed Lockhart on the lips before backing away to look into his eyes.

He spied her broad smile then met her gaze. "What was that for?"

"For," she glimpsed the landscape behind Baxter's house then spied Lockhart again, "for going back for Ranger."

He returned to the dog in question, draped his left arm around the GSD's shoulders, then patted his K-9 deputy's chest. "Of course, I went back for him. I'd never leave a man behind. Right, bud?"

With Sierra looking on, and smiling the whole time, Lockhart and Ranger roughhoused with each other, each one giving as good as he got.

Two days ago, Lockhart and Piper had traveled to a neighboring state. Then, in the early evening hours, with assistance from local law enforcement, they had arrested the man who Baxter Nash had initially hired to set up the contract killing of Jace Lockhart.

With the last person involved in the conspiracy in custody, Lockhart had decided to take a couple days off, leaving his undersheriff in charge. Of course, he had left her with instructions to call him if anything serious came up. As the sheriff of Big Sky County, he knew he was never truly off the clock.

Today, his second day off, had been a laid-back kind of day. Lockhart, Sierra, and Ranger had spent time lounging around the house before taking a long walk in the woods near his home. A good game of 'toss the stick' with Ranger, while Lockhart and Sierra had strolled along, holding hands, had proved therapeutic for the couple, helping them get back to what really mattered in life.

Now, with Sierra out shopping, Lockhart had

retreated to his home's attic, Ranger in tow. With tongue-and-groove wooden floors and a finished ceiling, the attic was a clean and ordered storage space. Everything stored here was either on a shelf or stacked neatly against a wall or packed away in an old dresser or cabinet. Add a bed, and someone could sleep the night here.

In the center of the attic, on a nine-by-twelve-foot area rug—a plug-in space heater facing him and his furry companion—Wade Lockhart sat on an old wooden rocking chair beside a small table. An overhead light fixture hung from the ceiling, casting downward light around the space. On his left, Ranger laid on the rug with his head between his paws. With his legs crossed at the knee, his thoughts lost in the past, Lockhart stared at his favorite framed photo of his deceased wife Cheryl, of her all bundled up in a winter coat, snow falling around her, as she looked to the sky, her arms spread wide as the camera had caught her in mid spin. He had always thought this image perfectly captured her free and loving spirit. His memories turned to what she had said to him the night of her fatal accident, minutes before her passing...

"I know you, Wade," said Cheryl. "You're a thinker," despite her pain, she chuckled, "sometimes to your own detriment."

Tears streaming down his face, Lockhart half

laughed, too.

Cheryl cupped his cheek, wiping his tears with her thumb. "Remember me, my love, but don't let," she closed her eyes and took a strained breath, trying to tamp down her discomfort, before opening them again and giving him a warm smile, "but don't let a memory keep you from moving on. You *have* to move on." She then gave him a Bible verse and asked him to read it often.

Lockhart laid the photo on his lap, picked up a Bible, and opened the book to Jeremiah twenty-nine to read verse eleven to himself. *For I know well the plans I have in mind for you, plans for your welfare and not for woe, so as to give you a future of hope.* He read the verse four more times before closing the Bible and exchanging it for the picture of Cheryl.

Following another five minutes of admiring her, he rocked forward, stood, and strolled to a dresser, Jace's dresser from his teenage years. He laid the frame in a cardboard box on the dresser; on top of several other photo frames in the box, pictures Lockhart had recently gathered from around his house. All were of Wade and Cheryl, Cheryl and Jace, or Wade, Cheryl, and their son.

Opening the dresser's top drawer, he saw the left half filled with old greeting cards Cheryl had saved. "How do you throw these away?" she had asked him on many occasions. His response had been, "They've served their purpose. Time to let them go." He had never understood how she could keep so many cards, a great number of them from decades ago.

Lockhart placed the box of photos next to the stack of greeting cards while saying under his breath, "I get it now, Cheryl. I get it." He then hung his head and recalled the Bible verse she had asked him to read. Sniffing once, he nodded at the floor. "And I think I understand what you were trying to tell me, too. I will nev—"

"Wade?" came a female voice from downstairs.

Ranger's ears went up before he trotted across the room and tiptoed down the wooden stairs.

Lockhart hauled out a handkerchief from his pocket. He dried his eyes before running the cloth over his nose. "I will never forget you," he said to the image. "But I also know it's time for me to," he swallowed, Cheryl's words to him—from that night—playing in his head, as he said them aloud, "to move on."

He put his fingers to his lips, touched his late wife's face in the photo, then gave her a last look before slowly closing the dresser door.

Ranger returned.

Seconds later, Sierra came up the stairs. "There you are." She glanced around the attic. "What're you doing up here?"

Lockhart shoved his handkerchief into a jean pocket and met her at the stairs.

She thought she noticed redness in his eyes. *Has he been cry—*

He embraced her.

Surprised, she held her arms out at her sides for a second before hugging him back. "Are you o—"

He clinched her tighter.

"Oomph," grunted Sierra.

Moments later, after planting a long kiss on her right cheek, Lockhart pulled away but held her in his arms.

She frowned at him then half smiled. "What was *that* for?"

He pressed his lips together then reached up to push a lock of hair away from her face. "No reason."

She observed him. "Are you okay?"

Interlacing his fingers at the small of her back, his brows converging, "I," he mulled over her query then nodded, "I think I am. Yes." Two pulses later, he poked his chin at her. "Were you able to get everything we needed from the store?"

Sierra cocked her head at him, her mind trying to read him. In the next instant, she blinked a few times then rubbed her palms up and down his upper arms. "Yes, I was. Everything's waiting for us in the kitchen."

"Great. Let's get started." Lockhart took her by the hand and led her down the stairs, Ranger slipping by on the sheriff's left and darting through the door below.

· · ·

Two Hours Later...
"I'd love to help you with the dishes, Wade, but duty

calls." Sitting on the loveseat in the sunken area of the living room, facing the gas fireplace in the northwest corner, with Ranger laying curled up in front of the fire, his backside to the heat, Sierra took the bottle of warm milk from Kinsley. "Thank you." She positioned Jace Wade just right then began feeding him.

Lockhart half smiled at his girlfriend while stacking plates and silverware. Having invited Kinsley and JW to dinner two days ago, Lockhart and Sierra had spent the last two hours cooking a homemade meal. Now, with everyone's belly full, except for JW's, the only work left to do was to clean up the mess.

"Are you sure you're okay with this?" asked Kinsley.

"Are you kidding? I'm in my glory here."

The younger woman beamed. "I'll go help with the dishes, then." Bypassing the kitchen table, she scooped up three cups, a tub of butter, and the pan of mashed potatoes. Deftly navigating around chairs, she took the cups to the sink, then put the butter in the fridge, before turning toward Lockhart. "What should I do with the potatoes?"

Unbuttoning his shirt sleeves, he motioned toward the counter. "Just put it there. I'll take care of them later."

She put the pan down and eyed the dirty dishes. "Can I help with anything?"

He shook his head. "These won't take long."

She dipped her head, nodded once, then spun around.

He noticed the sudden change in her demeanor, and Bristol's observations, her advice, came racing back to him. *She's definitely trying to find out where she stands with you. Pay attention to the signs, and you'll see what I'm seeing.* "Uh, Kinsley?"

She pivoted back toward him. "Yes?"

He folded a shirt sleeve up his forearm. "I just wanted you to know that," a beat, "I'm not trying to overstep my bounds here, but," another beat, "but if you ever need someone to," he tipped his head from side to side, "I don't know...drive a nail, turn a screw, or, or," he shrugged a shoulder, "fix a leaky faucet..."

She nodded.

"Well," he started working on his second sleeve, "well, I want you to feel comfortable enough to know that you can call on me for help."

Kinsley smiled.

"I'm here for JW, but I'm also here for *you*. Okay?"

She bobbed her head up and down a couple times. "Thank you. I will. Call you if I need help, that is."

Lockhart nodded. "Okay. Good." He plugged the sink drain, turned on the faucet, then squeezed soap into the basin. Out of the corner of his eye, he saw her moving toward him. Thinking she was coming in for a hug, he stood taller.

Kinsley pivoted toward the counter and threw her left hip into him. "Now beat it," her voice dipped almost to a whisper, "Pop," before returning to its normal volume, "and let me do these, will you?"

The faucet had been running full blast and pelting the stainless-steel, but he was almost certain he had heard the fatherly moniker Jace had always used. A sea of happy memories flooding his brain, he inwardly smiled.

"Besides," she shut off the faucet and dipped the first dish into the standing water, "I think JW wants to spend some quality time with his grandfather."

Lifting a corner of his mouth, Lockhart nodded once, draped a dish towel over her right shoulder, then squeezed her other shoulder twice. "Okay. I can take a hint."

Kinsley watched him leave before looking down at her work. A moment later, with her lips curling upward, she tilted her head to the left and rubbed her cheek across the spot he had touched, her heart still feeling the tender presses he had given her.

— Thank You —

Thank you for purchasing and reading *RECKONING*. I hope you enjoyed the third installment, as well as the first two books, in the BIG SKY series of modern sheriff crime thrillers. Keep reading for a sneak peek at *EXECUTIVE ONE FOXTROT*, a patriotic action thriller.

Blessings and Peace,

Alex

P.S. If you haven't downloaded your FREE ebook, *Escape & Evade*, at my website (AlexAnderNovelist.com), it's still waiting for you.

EXECUTIVE ONE FOXTROT

A PATRIOTIC ACTION THRILLER

ALEX ANDER

CHAPTER 1
THE FIRST LADY

The weight bearing down on the First Lady of the United States was suffocating, like being at the bottom of the pile after a fourth-and-inches goal line stand. She had never considered herself claustrophobic. But having been shoved to the Chevy Suburban's floorboards between the backseat and the front seat's upright, her left cheek pressing on a dirty floor mat, FLOTUS was now having second thoughts about that self-assessment. Plus, the two-hundred-plus-pound man pinning her to the floor only added to her fears.

The speeding SUV hit a bump, forcing the man on top of her to rise into the air a fraction of an inch. She was able to steal a half breath before the heavyweight came back down again, the man's momentum compressing her upper body even more.

Moments ago, or *minutes* ago—since it's hard to tell time when you're struggling to breathe and can't see anything but carpet fibers and the metal workings beneath the driver's seat—the mad dash to the motorcade had been chaotic.

• • •

Minutes ago...

"In closing," said the First Lady, standing behind a makeshift podium and speaking to a small crowd of Panamanians who looked as ragged and worn out as the weather-ravaged countryside surrounding the gathering, "I'd like to take this opportunity to assure you, the citizens of Panama, that," she glanced at her hand-written remarks, "the United State—"

Deafening booms and ear-splitting cracks interrupted the speech, shattering the atmosphere of an otherwise peaceful evening.

Shouting and screaming, people ducked and ran for cover.

In an instant, FLOTUS was surrounded by men in black suits. A hand clamped around the back of her neck and pushed her head downward. Her notes went flying, and all the First Lady could now make out were the shiny dress shoes of her Secret Service detail. In fact, she wasn't really sure she was even in control of her footsteps as the agents were seemingly carrying her.

The barrage of gunshots continued unceasingly, coming from all directions.

FLOTUS heard the shouts, the cries of civilians caught in the crossfire, the grunts coming from the men around her. One by one, after each muffled groan, a pair of black dress shoes near her disappeared from her vision.

Twice her armed escorts veered off course and took cover—shielding FLOTUS with their bodies—only to yank her to her feet a second later, their pistols barking, as the diamond formation, with the First Lady in the center, rushed forward.

"Shooter—ten o'clock."

Gunfire.

"Three o'clock! Three o'clock!"

More gunfire.

"Threat down. Go, go, go!"

"Sunflower on the move."

"Eight o'clock. White truck. Front bum—" a loud groan came before a pair of shoes disappeared.

"Engaging."

Gunfire.

"Threat dow—" a moan came before another set of shoes disappeared.

"Robbins, take left flank," shouted the man 'glued' to the First Lady.

Shoes came into view on her left as she glimpsed an SUV up ahead.

"Fall back and—" her 'shadow' let loose with three rounds from his pistol.

The First Lady flinched every time the weapon fired.

"Fall back and establish perimeter."

Seconds later, her world went dark when she was pushed into the SUV and shoved face first to the floor, the man on her immediate left throwing himself on top of her. The vehicle was rolling before she saw the right-rear door slam shut.

• • •

Present time...

Now, several starts and stops and sharp turns later, with the Secret Service agent draped over her, crushing her upper body, FLOTUS did her best at a one-handed push-up. With her left arm wedged under her, she drove her left elbow downward. Both actions allowed her to gain some separation from the floor, and she grabbed a scant breath before gravity and lack of muscle strength once again forced her back down. Unable to fill her lungs, panic sunk in. Perspiration dotted her forehead. A deep thirst gripped at the back of her throat. And her chest felt like it was collapsing, as she labored for more oxygen, heck, *any* oxygen.

The SUV rolled to a halt then lurched backward a few seconds ahead of the left-rear door swinging open.

FLOTUS lifted her eyes to see another black-suited man wrestling with the one covering her. Seconds later, the heavy load was gone, and she rolled right to get her first full breath in who knows how long.

Strong hands slipped under her armpits.

Hoisted upward, she was dragged out of the vehicle, her chunky high heels scraping across the floorboards, before she was placed on her feet.

• • •

Ten seconds earlier...

The driver threw the gearshift into 'PARK,' pushed open his door, and clambered outside, his peripheral vision picking up on the smoke billowing from the front of the SUV while he drew his Glock G19 Gen5 MOS pistol. He opened the left-rear door, his head on a swivel, his eyes taking in every detail behind the boarded-up supermarket, wood coverings on windows being the owner's last-ditch attempt at saving his property from the tropical storm that had recently ravaged the area.

Moments later, he looked down to see a motionless Secret Service agent lying on the First Lady.

The prone man's black suit coat had two holes in it, two darker, circular patches growing wider.

The driver holstered his weapon then wrestled to roll his fellow agent onto the backseat. After checking the man for vital signs, and finding none, he slid his hands under the woman's armpits, hauled her out of the SUV, and gently set her on her feet. "Are you all right, Mrs. Conklin? Are you injured? Are you feeling any pain anywhere?" he said, all the while inspecting her for obvious signs of physical trauma.

Based on the powerful arms that had lifted her from the vehicle, Caroline Conklin had anticipated having to crane her neck at someone towering above her five-three height. Instead, she found herself only a couple inches shy of her rescuer. Granted, the difference was skewed by her three-inch black high heels, however.

The late-forties woman straightened her rumpled navy-blue pantsuit before unbuttoning the jacket to inspect her white blouse underneath. "I-I don't think so." She quickly ran fingers through her shoulder-length strawberry blonde hair, pushing aside the wavy locks that blocked her vision.

"Good." Removing his black sunglasses, the man took her by the right elbow and led her away from the disabled ride. "We should get going." With one hand, he folded the spectacles then stuffed them into a pocket on his black suit coat.

"Why not take the car?"

"It took a round in the radiator. It barely had enough power to get us this far."

The two fast walked toward the corner of the single-story building, Caroline's heels clicking and scuffing as she did her best to keep up with her guide's pace. She glanced back. "Where are the others? There were three cars in the motorcade."

"One vehicle was disabled. I'm not sure about the third."

Caroline frowned while recalling all the pairs of shoes that had disappeared from her vision during the race to the SUV. Her heart sunk when she turned back to see the motionless agent who had been lying on top of her. Knowing the answer to her next question, she asked anyway. "What," she faltered, "what about the others...the men who were with you?"

They made a hard left then navigated a narrow alley before emerging onto a sidewalk.

"Many of them fell during the gunfight," said the man. "Those left standing stayed behind to give us time to escape." The Secret Service agent dug out his cell phone and saw that he had no cellular service.

Caroline slowed and thrust out her left arm to steady herself on the building. A tick later, she bent over and put her free hand to her stomach.

The agent whirled around and dashed to her side. "Ma'am?"

She waved him off then wiped sweat from her forehead. "It's all right. I'm fine. I just," she swallowed, hoping to keep the bile in her throat from advancing any further, "I just suddenly feel sick to my stomach." She made a face and blinked several times, moisture gathering at the corners of her eyes. "All those men." She shook her head and sniffed before using her fingers to clear away the tears. "All those men."

"Those men would have died a *thousand* deaths to protect Sunflower. That's our job, our calling. It's what we're trained for."

Caroline heard the call sign that had been assigned to her. With her daughter's call sign being Red Rose, she was pleased that the Secret Service had stayed with the flower theme. And it just so happened that sunflowers were near the top of her list when it came to her favorites. "I know." Caroline nodded. "I know. But it's still hard to wrap my head around good people dying so that I might live." She sniffled again then swiped fingers over her nose.

His head spinning left and right, the agent retrieved a white handkerchief from a trouser pocket and held it out to her while looking up and repeating his scanning procedure.

Caroline accepted the offering. "Thank you."

"You're welcome, Ma'am." He continued surveying the empty street before glancing up to take in the upper windows and rooftops. "We need to keep moving, get off the street. I know a place, a block over, where we can hide for the time being."

She dried her eyes and nose with the cloth then nodded. "I'm ready."

He claimed her elbow again.

"Sorry for being such a wimp."

The two hurried forward.

"You're not a wimp, Ma'am. It's called having a big heart. And it's one of the reasons why I'm honored—why *all of us*—are honored to have the opportunity to safeguard you."

They jogged across the street.

Caroline threw out her right leg, half leaping for the

curb and half trying to keep up with the agent. Her heel skidded over the raised concrete. Her right ankle twisted a bit, and she wobbled, her right knee buckling. "Oh, sh…"

He caught her as she finished her curse in his left ear. "I got you. You're good."

She regained her balance and half smiled at him. "I'm sorry. That wasn't very," a beat, "*first* ladylike of me."

"I've heard much worse, Ma'am." He dipped his chin at her. "You ready?"

She nodded.

The two fast walked down a narrow side street, dodging broken bottles, tipped-over trash cans, and a mound of something black and mushy to which both people gave a wide berth.

Veering right and stooping, the agent snagged a two-foot length of rusted pipe.

"What's that for?" asked Caroline, her brows coming together.

"I'm thinking I might need a persuader."

"A persuader?"

"We're almost there, Ma'am." Exiting the side street, he ushered her to the left then pulled on a door handle.

The door didn't budge.

"Stand back, Ma'am."

FLOTUS backtracked a couple feet.

On his second swing of the pipe, he shattered a window on the door. Using the steel conduit, he cleared away the rest of the shards, stuck an arm inside the opening, and unlocked the door. After stepping inside, he backed out and motioned. "After you, Mrs. Conklin. The way's clear."

She spied the 'persuader' he held then proffered a half grin while bypassing her protector. "From what I'm told, my husband could use a *persuasive* man like you at his cabinet meetings."

The agent surveyed the surrounding area. Satisfied no one was watching, he slipped into the building and shut the door.

9 798230 525233